I0535935

HOW TO SAVE A
SURGEON

A GAMBLING HEARTS STORY

C.M. STONE

This book is a work of fiction. Names, characters, places, and incidents are the product of the author's imagination or are used fictitiously. Any resemblance to actual events, locales, or persons, living or dead, is coincidental.

Copyright © 2015 by C.M. Stone. All rights reserved, including the right to reproduce, distribute, or transmit in any form or by any means. For information regarding subsidiary rights, please contact the Publisher.

Entangled Publishing, LLC
2614 South Timberline Road
Suite 109
Fort Collins, CO 80525
Visit our website at www.entangledpublishing.com.

Lovestruck is an imprint of Entangled Publishing, LLC.

Edited by Heather Howland and Vanessa Mitchell
Cover design by Heather Howland
Cover art by Reed Files

Manufactured in the United States of America

First Edition July 2015

To India, my fashion montage buddy. Absolutely everybody needs a good friend, a bottle of wine, and a closet full of dress up clothes.

Chapter One

Darla wasn't late, though part of her wished she had been. Nerves over working with a new surgeon in the UMC Trauma Center had sent her rushing through her morning, and she'd arrived to wait for him two minutes early.

Two minutes to spend doing nothing but standing around stuck in her own head. It was better than ten minutes of waiting, at least, but she still found herself anxiously rocking on her heels.

"Wait," a man's deep voice echoed from down the hall. "Does McGaffey think *I* lack patience?"

Her head automatically turned toward the indignant tone. The man who'd spoken was looking at the Chief of Trauma Medicine, his face tense and guarded as if expecting an unpleasant answer.

Chief Singh just smiled, then pointed toward Darla. "There's your new intern."

The man standing beside the Chief of Trauma Medicine

jerked his head in her direction. Dr. Jackson DeMatteo. Her new mentor. The man who would determine her fate in trauma medicine.

Lots of people had warned her that he was a nightmare. Demanding. Relentlessly focused on the job. That he had the highest, most stringent standards of any doctor any of them had ever had to work with. Other residents often called him Dr. Ice behind his back. There was plenty of talk about his work ethic, but her peers failed to mention that the man was gorgeous. He stood a little over six feet tall with broad shoulders and smooth, tanned skin. His rich brown hair was clipped short and neat, ideal for a physician. His light green eyes were fringed with thick black lashes—of course they were—making for a stark contrast against his dark, Mediterranean good looks. His full lips pursed in a frown, and she noticed a faint little dimple in his chin.

Great. She was gawking. As that realization struck her, she dropped her eyes and stepped forward to offer him her hand. "Dr. DeMatteo, I-I've heard amazing things about you. I'm Darla Morales, and I'm really excited to be working with you."

"And you actually requested to work with me, too," DeMatteo pointed out as he accepted her hand. The tension in his face eased, his full lips curving into a faint, puzzled smile. "Why is that?"

The friendly question sparked unexpected confidence in her, which she eagerly latched on to. The lust he was inspiring, on the other hand, wasn't as helpful. She took a deep breath, trying to recall the answer she'd rehearsed for his question, and did her best to ignore the scent of DeMatteo's aftershave. It smelled like spice and cedar.

"I'm about to finish up my first year, and then I want to begin a specialty track residency in trauma medicine. Mc-Gaffey had been my first choice for a mentor here, but since she's retiring in a few weeks she suggested that I speak to you instead."

DeMatteo rose both of his brows slightly at that, then turned to give a smug look to the chief before turning back to her. "That's fantastic. She was my mentor when I first began my specialty track. I'd be honored to continue her fine tradition."

They stepped away a bit from the chief and another doctor who had been hovering nearby. At the moment, she was still trying to find the right balance of eye contact with DeMatteo, so she didn't give much attention to anyone else. She was vaguely aware that the chief was watching them, though.

"Everyone has to spend at least some of their first year in the trauma center, so I imagine you've gotten a basic grounding in trauma already, but it really is a far more complex specialty than most people from outside the field can appreciate," DeMatteo said.

That earlier confidence bubbled forth. "I know. My mother's worked as a trauma nurse pretty much all my life."

He paused and his smile faded, making her heart sink. "Be careful. Don't say you know something you don't. I'm sure your mother is a very good nurse, but right now you're a first-year surgical intern. You don't actually know what it's like inside the field."

"But I've been living and breathing this since I was seven." The dwindling warmth in his face was sending off little warnings all through her brain, but she forged ahead.

"I know I'm just an intern, but I've read so much in preparation. While my roommate was playing Call of Duty this morning, I was reading about sexual dimorphism in trauma."

Instead of being impressed with her, he was looking more exasperated by the moment. "There's no proven sexual dimorphism in trauma."

"No! There is. It's been studied for years and years, even. It affects immune and organ responsiveness. The susceptibility to and morbidity from shock, trauma, and sepsis is worse in men, because female hormones actually have a protective effect. By using estrogen treatment, it could potentially reduce morbidity for men."

He pinched the bridge of his nose, eyes closed. "We don't give estrogen to men after trauma just because there's a theorized sex difference. That's…that sounds dangerously stupid. Where are you getting this?"

"It was in this paper I was reading this morning." Darla pulled out her phone and began searching for it, almost frantic now. He had just called her stupid. Or, well, he had called what she was saying stupid. The need to prove herself was overriding every bit of sense she had. "Here! See? It was observed in rats and the results were reproduced in humans, going back almost twenty years."

He drew his hand back from his face to take her phone. She watched as his eyes scanned the document she'd loaded. Instead of looking pleased at learning something new, he only sighed.

"Twenty years," he said.

She nodded, feeling a bit like a bobble head doll with the rapidity of the motion. "It goes back to the mid-nineties, at least. I'm surprised you graduated without ever hearing about it, actually."

"You're surprised I graduated medical school without knowing about an experimental hormone treatment that no one is using?" Irritation practically dripped off of his words, and she finally got a sense of just how far she had pushed things. The first rule of holes, she knew, was to stop digging. Figuring out how to do that was the hard part.

"No. No, of course not," she said. "I just would've expected you to know that female patients tolerate blood loss and recover from sepsis better. That's really common knowledge, isn't it?"

He dropped her phone back into her hand, then shook his head slightly before walking away from her. The full enormity of her blunder struck her like a piano dropping off a roof. Her diaphragm started to squeeze painfully with every breath as her heart pounded in her ears. One of the rising stars at the hospital, certainly someone well-connected to just about everyone above her, and she had just argued with him publicly and essentially called him ignorant. What the *hell* had she been thinking? Why couldn't she have gotten tongue-tied or just been speechless in terror instead of babbling like an absolute ass?

Before she could start crying or do anything worse to add to the horror of the situation, she dashed away. Part of her wanted to just keep running all the way back home.

Jackson stepped a few feet away as he attempted to gather his thoughts. Showing the chief that he was talented at teaching became a far more difficult task when his newest intern was trying to school him. Snapping at her out of embarrassment would hardly help his efforts to look like good professor material, but the urge was high. Finding a more diplomatic way to explain how medical consensus worked and that a few studies weren't enough to make sweeping declarations seemed best. Or it did until he heard feet running. He turned to watch as she fled.

"Fuck," he swore under his breath.

Another surgeon had lingered to watch the exchange and asked in a falsetto, "Oh, Dr. DeMatteo, how could you possibly not know about sexual dimorphism in trauma?"

"Shut up, Mevlyn." Jackson dragged a hand through his hair, thinking. She seemed to know her material well enough—it was true that he'd never heard anyone suggest using hormone therapy on male trauma patients—but there was more to being a trauma surgeon than collecting theories. Still, if she could keep from running away it might even be fun to debate things with her. Provided she didn't start it up in front of the chief.

"That didn't last very long," Chief Singh pointed out dryly. "I expected you to at least get through a single shift with her."

"I didn't chase her off." He pointed in the direction she'd run. "That was all her."

"Yes, I heard." The chief gave him a little smile. "And I didn't hear you reeling her in and getting her back on track."

"How the hell could I? She barely gave me a chance to get a word in edgewise before she was ranting on about some bullshit estrogen therapy somebody dreamed up in the nineties."

That little smile vanished from the chief's face. "It's not

bullshit. I had provided some patient data for one of those studies."

Kill me now, Jackson silently prayed.

"I'll find her and get her back in the trauma center," he said, desperate to change the subject. "She's pretty high-strung, though. I don't know how long she'll last."

"She'd better last through her residency."

Jackson felt as if ice water had just trickled down his spine. He stared at the chief for a moment, trying to determine if the older man was joking or not, but he looked perfectly serious. "You want me to keep her in here for years?"

The chief spread his hands, shrugging. "At least until she's chosen her specialty. Morales is nearly done with her first year now, after all, so you don't have that long to hold her hand until she's on a specialty track. How well she does from that point will be up to her, but I expect her to stick with trauma."

The horror of it all crept up on him. "She couldn't last five minutes. Literally, just now? That was less than five minutes."

"I'm aware of how long it was, DeMatteo. Are you aware of how you could have handled it better?"

"I don't know. Made her shut up sooner?" As was too often the case, his sarcastic sense of humor went unappreciated.

The chief gave him a sour look, then shook his head. "You're the experienced attending surgeon here. You could have kept your ego in check, instead of getting defensive when she pointed out you were wrong."

Jackson bit his tongue to keep from arguing. He hadn't been wrong. Whatever a handful of studies said, there was no consensus on the topic. Until there was consensus, he had no reason to revise the standard medical assumptions he'd been taught.

"Make a trauma surgeon out of her, DeMatteo," Singh continued. "Show me you have what it takes to be responsible for molding future doctors."

That caught his attention. He glanced in the direction Morales had run, then turned back to the chief. "That's it? That's what you want from me for McGaffey's position? Make Morales a useful member of the trauma team?"

It was a running joke among the other adjunct faculty in the medical school that it was easier to kill a tenured professor and get their position than wait for one of the positions to open up. For an ambitious young surgeon like him, getting a shot at professorship instead of only being an instructor could be the difference between a career and just having a job. McGaffey's retirement from teaching was the opportunity he'd been waiting for.

"Do you think you can do it?"

Jackson opened his mouth to answer, then paused. The desire to answer in the affirmative was overpowering, but was it true? While McGaffey must have seen something in Morales to actually recommend he mentor her, it was difficult to gauge her strengths yet. They had only spoken for a moment. One hell of a moment.

"Of course he can't," Mevlyn cut in. "He can't even get a normal intern to stick around. How could DeMatteo possibly manage with a walking panic attack like that?"

That made the decision for him. Jackson snapped his mouth shut and shot a glare in Mevlyn's direction. "She's a nervous first-year resident. Cut her some slack."

She *had* been nervous. He'd recognized that, but he'd let

his frustration with her babbling get the better of him. Her big brown eyes had been so wide behind her glasses, and she'd pulled her black curls into an impossibly tight ponytail with them exploding into a puff behind her head, making her heart-shaped face look younger and smaller. Not all of her had looked so delicate, though. Even with the top of her head barely reaching his shoulder, her body was full and rounded with tempting curves.

He pushed those unprofessional thoughts away and refocused on the chief. "I can do it. She's bright and clearly driven. It's just a matter of directing that well."

Singh relaxed and a smile returned to his face once more. "You think you can direct her?"

"I know I can."

Mevlyn crossed his arms. "You're really going to offer him McGaffey's tenure track position for getting one intern to be quasi-functional?"

"It's not my place to offer it. Those decisions are decided by the medical school board," the chief corrected. "I can make recommendations, though, as will McGaffey."

"And what happens when he fails? Who's your backup recommendation?" Mevlyn pressed.

Jackson held his breath, though he knew what the answer would be. Instead of actually saying it out loud, the chief only gave Mevlyn a knowing look. The other man had a few more years of experience than Jackson, and even if he was one of the laziest instructors Jackson had ever heard of, he knew how to play hospital politics.

"Morales is going to be a trauma surgeon," Jackson told the chief firmly. "There's no other way I'll let this end."

Chapter Two

The supply closet wasn't the most dignified place to hide, but it was the first and most private location Darla had seen. She shifted on the plastic tote she'd chosen as her seat and hugged her knees to her chest, trying to bring her breathing under control. It was out of proportion to what happened, and she knew it, yet logic had little to do with her anxiety. Her brain had settled into a feedback loop of horror as she ran through the conversation over and over again.

What had she been thinking? So he was wrong about something. So he didn't read journals as closely as she did. Telling him that he was wrong in front of everyone was no way to help matters. It certainly hadn't made him listen to her.

"I hate everything and everyone, especially me," she muttered to herself as she hugged her knees.

"That sounds pretty dire for a little argument."

She looked up at the voice and saw Jackson DeMatteo

standing in the doorway of the supply closet. With her heart pounding in her ears, she hadn't noticed the door opening. A wave of horror washed over her, leaving her head feeling so light she feared she was going to pass out. That was all she needed, dropping at his feet.

"Dr. DeMatteo," she said in a rush as she scrambled to stand. "I'm so sorry. I shouldn't—"

"Wait." He held a hand up to her, his other hand shutting the door behind him. "I don't care about your apology."

Her stomach clenched, and she thought she could taste bile on the back of her tongue. Vomiting at his feet might be worse than fainting. "You don't?"

"No. I don't need you to grovel. I just need you to put effort into this and make it work. Are you going to do that?"

Her heart leaped and she worried she might get a headache from the mood whiplash. "Yes, yes, absolutely," she insisted. "Thank you so much."

His full lips pressed together in frown. God, he was even sexy when he was frowning at her. Not making a complete idiot over herself moment by moment was going to be far harder than any surgery she had ever assisted on.

"Don't thank me. Just do what's required. Why are you interested in trauma medicine?"

"My mom's a trauma nurse."

DeMatteo raised one brow slightly, then gave her a prompting gesture. "And?"

Had that been the wrong answer? Whenever she had mentioned her family history in medicine, everyone else had simply accepted it happily. It seemed like the motivation for a lot of high-achievers, too. Darla struggled to elaborate. "And I want to be like her?"

"Why?"

Her scalp was prickling with sweat under all of the hairspray she'd put on that morning. Why weren't her answers good enough for him? Was he just being sadistic to get back at her for earlier? "I...admire my mother?"

"I was looking for answers, not more questions. Don't ask me why you're doing it," he said. "Can I give you a word of advice? Our parents make for really shitty motivators in life. Yeah, they love us, but they think they know us better than they really do. You need to do this for you, not your mother."

"I...I am doing it for me?" Shit. She was making it sound like a question again. Darla shook her head, warding off another correction from him. "I've always wanted to be a doctor and surgeons seemed like gods to me when I was a kid. My dad—"

"Don't put your motivations on your parents," DeMatteo cut in gently.

Her mouth snapped shut, and she breathed in deeply before she tried again. "My dad died from an undiagnosed heart problem when I was three. I'd like to save people like him."

It was DeMatteo's turn to be silenced, and he even had the good grace to look embarrassed. After a moment, he nodded. "So why not cardiology?"

She shrugged. "It just doesn't interest me."

"Then you should follow your interests."

Was trauma her biggest interest? The thought unsettled her because an answer didn't come to her as easily as it should have, but she couldn't dwell long. DeMatteo was already moving on. "Do this to help people, Morales. Not to impress anyone, not to make them happy. You'll always be disappointed if you're trying to live up to somebody else's dream, but every day, even if you lose a patient, you can help."

Darla breathed a bit easier with that small measure of his approval. Whatever he wanted to say about not doing things to make other people happy, it rang a touch hollow when she had to work so hard for the smallest bit of acceptance. "I take it your parents aren't surgeons?"

DeMatteo shook his head. "No. My mom's a high school teacher and my dad's a professor of philosophy."

"Oh. So you didn't have any real urge to follow in their footsteps?"

"Not really." After he said it, he got a thoughtful look on his face as though something had just occurred to him. "I'm a part-time instructor for the medical school, and I would like to be a professor, but that's more about advancing my medical career than anything. If I want to be the Chief of Trauma Medicine someday, I need to be a tenured professor first."

She cocked her head in interest and stepped a little closer to the door. The threat of hyperventilating or crying was over, so there was less reason to hide out in the supply closet with him. Not unless he had a thing for supply closets or something, in which case she'd try not to judge.

"That's your goal? To replace the chief?"

"When he retires. I've got a five year plan so I can be in position for it before he leaves."

"That's fantastic!" she beamed. With such lofty goals, who could blame him for maybe being a little intense about his work? "I'm all about plans."

"And where will you be in five years?"

She paused, hissing inward through her teeth. Telling him that she was planning on leaving Las Vegas for her specialty track would likely not go over well. Several other interns had warned her that saying anything before she had the program director's permission would look bad. No one demanded it, but there was an unspoken assumption that staying with the same hospital through all the years of training was proper.

"Competing with you," she said.

He laughed and gave her a little nod of respect before he moved to open the door. "You're lucky your first rotation with me is in the morning. Things tend to be at their quietest in the trauma center at this time of day."

She stepped into the hall behind him. "Not getting any experience doesn't sound very lucky to me."

"You ever have to deal with the aftermath of a drive-by?"

Her heart started to pound just at the thought. "No."

"Let's just say it wouldn't be the best way to start your trauma education, then."

He pulled his phone out of his pocket to look at while they walked, scrolling and muttering beneath his breath. She wanted to ask what his phone had done to make him so angry, but wisely bit it back. Better not to do anything more to aggravate him.

Despite DeMatteo's warnings of a quiet morning, they only made it through checking on two patients before he was paged to the ambulance bay. He paused long enough to take off his white coat and be helped into a surgical gown over his suit, then rushed out to meet the ambulance. His speed and the way he just ran through everything as if it came to him automatically only heightened her awareness of her every fumble. Following him felt like trying to chase after a rabbit in an obstacle course.

When she finally caught up, Chief Singh was already briefing the other teams. "—wall collapsed with three construction workers on it, so be prepared for fall and crush injuries. They got it from all sides."

The first patient off an ambulance went to DeMatteo and her. The blur of the EMTs running through his injuries and DeMatteo barking instructions as they rushed the gurney inside filled her head with memories of facts and diagrams and skill lab practice. For a moment, she felt confident in it all. It was just a matter of remembering things and doing them well. That moment ended the second she actually saw the patient.

The man was in a collar to protect his neck and looked like he'd been beaten by bricks, which made sense if a wall had collapsed on him. They cut away his shirt to get at his injuries, revealing black bruises across his chest and stomach that perfectly matched textbook descriptions. She'd even seen identical photographs.

What she hadn't seen was a grown man inches away from her, sobbing that he couldn't feel his legs.

She blinked rapidly, trying to make the tears stop before anyone else saw them, and backed up a step. Just an ordinary day at work and then here he was, battered and facing his life possibly changing forever. Or ending.

"Morales, I need you to—" DeMatteo cut himself off as he focused on her. He pressed his lips together in a grim line. "Step outside."

She took a deep, slightly shaky breath. "No, I'm fine!"

"Outside. Now."

Worse than being banished from the room would be making a scene. She gave him a curt nod, then stepped out. She paced back and forth in the hall, unsure of what to do with herself. There was always administrative work to do, but would he be angry if he couldn't find her?

After fifteen minutes, she decided that filing and checking charts was better than wasting the hospital's money by standing around. Angrily stabbing at a tablet touchscreen and reading kept her distracted too. Nearly two hours went by before Jackson was finished with the construction worker.

"Morales."

DeMatteo walked toward her as he pulled his white coat on again. The expression on his face was frustratingly neutral, giving nothing away.

"I would've been fine."

"I'm sure you would've, eventually. But it's not about you." He closed the distance between them and leaned down to speak quietly to her. His nearness made her stiffen, her skin tingling from the warmth he radiated. "Patients need to see us at our best, at all times. It's terrifying enough to be injured and in the hands of strangers. If they see you crying, that's going to make it that much worse for them."

Easy for him to say. Rather than argue, she clenched her teeth together and nodded. "And how is the patient?"

"Stable and unconscious. When he wakes up, we'll have a better idea of how well he'll recover." As close as he was, she noticed the tightness around his mouth and bone-deep weariness in his eyes for the first time. Stress wrapped around him like his white coat. He wasn't as unaffected as he acted.

She offered the tablet loaded with his charts to him. "I went through and prepared for the rest of your rounds."

"Good." Rather than take the charts from her right away, he pulled his phone out to check it again.

This time she couldn't fight her curiosity. "Are you waiting for something?"

He raised his eyes from the phone to meet hers and to her astonishment he actually turned a little red. "I was expecting a call from my parents about my birthday."

"Oh." She drew her brows together, looking around the hive of activity of the hospital. No one had said anything to him about it. Maybe she'd just missed the acknowledgment. "It's still early. Maybe they'll call around dinner time."

"They're on central time, so it's a little harder to schedule those things." He put his phone back, then took the charts from her. "And they forgot my birthday last year."

"Has anyone remembered?" After she blurted the question, she cringed. What the hell was wrong with her? Her day of absolute loserdom couldn't possibly get any worse, short of somehow lighting the hospital on fire and then falling in front of the firetruck naked.

Instead of looking offended or hurt by the question, DeMatteo gave her a small smile. "I'm having dinner with my sister and my best friend. I don't need people here to remember."

"But…" She trailed off, certain that saying anything more would only make things worse. It was his *birthday,* and he didn't expect any of his coworkers to remember. Worse than that, it didn't appear that any of them had. Or his parents.

She cleared her throat. "Happy birthday."

Chapter Three

The soft-spoken birthday wish from Morales barely registered as Jackson took the tablet. Not that he was trying to ignore her, but he couldn't let himself dwell on what day it was any longer. There were simply far more important things. Nothing that he had scheduled was pressing or especially helpful for her. Waiting for a case to come into the emergency room would be a crap shoot. Making her cry again wouldn't do any good.

Something twisted painfully in his gut at that thought.

"Thank you," he said when he realized how long he'd been silent. No, none of his current patients would help and it would just be cruel to throw a random crisis at her.

"We're going back to the emergency room." He handed over the tablet and began in that direction.

Even with her legs so much shorter than his, she kept pace with him without complaint. "Were you paged?"

"No. I'm going to find another case for you."

"What? Why?"

"Because you need it."

Once he'd made his way from the operating rooms to the trauma center, he found an intake nurse. The direst cases would be pushed through to see someone immediately, but there were always other cases. Patients whose lives weren't threatened might sit around for hours waiting for a doctor, which tended to make them understandably upset.

He lowered his voice when he spoke to the nurse, hoping Morales wouldn't overhear and be offended. "I need something easy."

"That sounds like a personal problem to me," the nurse remarked dryly, before directing him to the perfect patient.

A young couple in Vegas on their honeymoon had suffered a slight mishap, with the groom falling during rock climbing. A quick examination found most of his injuries superficial and trauma was minimal, except for the swelling in one arm. Normally it would be a simple matter of X-rays and dealing with the injury, but he had a fresh new wedding ring that wouldn't come off a now puffy finger.

"I don't want it cut off," the patient said, drawing his hand back protectively.

"Sweetie, it's just a ring," his wife reminded him.

"It'll be fine," Jackson said. "We've never had to cut a ring off in either of our medical careers. Morales here'll be able to save it for you." Out of the corner of his eye, he could see the mingled horror and confusion on Darla's face and ignored it. "Morales, why don't you go get the oxygen mask strap? The blunt-nosed thumb forceps you'll need are already here."

Darla stared at him a moment longer before walking

away. He half-expected her not to come back at all after the day she'd had so far, but she returned promptly with the strap he'd asked for. The materials assembled, he put a hand on her shoulder to guide her in front of him to face the patient.

"Start wrapping his ring finger with the strap so it overlaps itself and compresses the tissue slightly," he murmured into her ear. So close to her, he could feel the heat of her body clearly. Even if he'd closed his eyes, he could have pictured her curves perfectly with the way they fit against him. She must not have noticed just how little space she'd left between their bodies when she moved. He cleared his throat and backed up half a step.

Darla turned her head slightly to glance at him, then refocused on the patient and began following his instructions.

"Because the strap's flexible, it'll keep compressing even when you aren't pulling tight on it, but it'll have some give. Remember that. You won't want to use anything that isn't elastic," he went on.

Once she had the patient's finger wrapped up to the edge of the ring, Jackson handed her the forceps. "Push the end of the strap under the ring so you can pull it through. Then you're going to pull downward toward the end of his finger."

The swelling made pushing the strap under the ring more difficult than it would have been otherwise, but on her third try she got it through. As she pulled, the ring was pulled along with the strap, rotating around the man's finger like a corkscrew. The swelling was, at least temporarily, pressed down so the ring could move. As it got to the end of the patient's finger, it popped free and Jackson's hand shot out to catch it.

"Very impressive." He pressed the ring into her palm, feeling her fingers curl automatically to grip his hand. Heat coursed through his body from what should have been an innocent touch. Her hand was small in his and soft, good for delicate surgeries and so much more.

He drew his hand back with a jerk, desperate to shut down those unwanted thoughts. He forced himself to ignore Morales in favor of their patient. "Your wife can keep your wedding ring safe until you can wear it again. Why don't we get you up to radiology now?"

Busying himself getting the couple sent off for X-rays and paging orthopedics was all far safer than trying to figure out what the hell was wrong with him. Keeping personal feelings out of the workplace was one of the easiest boundaries he'd made for himself, yet Morales kept getting under his skin in unexpected ways. It didn't help that every step of the way as he tried to distract himself she was right there, watching and waiting.

"Why'd you drag me down here for that?" Her wide brown eyes sparkled with accomplishment that had been missing before, an eagerness to her face he'd only seen for a moment when they'd met earlier.

It felt good to see her that way again from a purely professional vantage point, but it only made her more appealing. Jackson grabbed the tablet again for something safer to look at. "What did you just learn?"

"How to remove a ring without cutting it."

"What else?"

A long moment passed before she spoke again, sounding less certain this time. "Almost lying to a patient. The only reason I haven't had to cut a ring off before is because I have hardly any experience yet—"

"You know how to avoid cutting them now, so you'll never have to cut a ring off," he interrupted. "But the point was you were compassionate without getting all wrapped up in your own feelings. You saved his ring, maybe even his finger if he'd kept refusing help."

She shook her head, making her pony tail swish back and forth. "It was just a ring."

"You ever been married, Morales? Or engaged?"

Her lips pursed in a small frown, drawing his attention to their tempting shape and fullness. "No."

All the rings he'd once looked at without ever buying one ran through his head. They were a good reminder of why it hurt too much to try again. Remembering that loss made it easy to return behind the walls he'd built.

"It's never just a ring." The words sound gruffer than he'd intended them, but maybe that was for the best.

The scent of homemade pesto hit Jackson the second he walked in the door. He closed his eyes and breathed deeply, instantly transported back to his childhood and Nonna DeMatteo's cooking. "Somebody must love me."

Chris appeared at the top of the stairs to grin down at him. "It's all your sister. I've got nothing to do with it."

The split-level condo had the kitchen, dining room, and living room on the upper level, with the two bedrooms on the lower. Both Chris and his sister had complained about the layout at various times, but the two of them kept normal hours in their careers. Jackson slept during the day frequently enough that having his bedroom partially underground was a godsend, particularly with the intense desert sunlight.

In the kitchen, he found his sister at the stove with a pot of pasta boiling. The food processor was still out on the counter with the pesto in it, a bowl with a half-finished salad next to it. Chris took the bottle of wine from Jackson to stick it in the fridge, then went back to his post at the sink where he was washing dishes. Likely the best place for him, considering some of his notorious failures at domesticity.

Eliza brushed back a curl that had escaped her bun to stick to her forehead and smiled. "Happy birthday. Cheesecake's cooking, and dinner should be done pretty fast."

"I can't believe you're actually cooking me dinner." Jackson gave his sister a quick kiss on the cheek, then inspected the salad bowl. "Is this Mom's spinach salad?"

"Yeah, I got a little behind on everything. I figured I could whip it together right before we ate."

"If you have the recipe, I'll finish it off. It's been a while since I cooked much but I'm pretty sure I can manage a salad."

Eliza nodded to the recipe notecard and gestured at Chris. "At least one of you can."

Chris only laughed. "Did she tell you about the popcorn?"

Jackson began slicing the red pepper into slivers for the salad. "What popcorn?"

"I brought my air popper out for movie night, and then there were a few unpopped kernels left in the bottom of the bowl. Chris put the bowl in the microwave to try to make them pop."

Jackson raised a brow at his best friend, waiting for an

explanation.

Chris grinned, clearly lacking any shame over the incident. "The bowl melted."

"Did the microwave survive?"

"Barely," Eliza said.

"Huh. Well. I'm glad you're the one cooking then."

"How was work?" Eliza asked.

He didn't relish the thought of reliving it all over again. Stumbling through the day with Morales was hard enough the first time. "Everyone's gearing up for the fund-raising gala this weekend. They're trying to get enough to expand the children's hospital. And I'm mentoring a new intern. Gonna try to get her to stay in trauma medicine, too. That's what the chief wants me to do, anyway."

The mirrored looks of dismayed shock from Eliza and Chris were downright insulting.

"That's a hell of a high bar, considering…" Chris said. "Does he want you to do it because of that professorship?"

He grabbed the bowl of salad and walked toward the table, buying himself some respite from the looks on their faces. Their concern wasn't anything he hadn't felt himself, but it seemed so much worse coming from them. "Yeah, and, yeah, I know. He thinks I need to prove myself, though."

"One-on-one isn't the same as a classroom," Eliza said. "Why not just go off your record as a surgeon and an instructor?"

There was no malice in their interest, even if it felt more like someone picking at a scab than idle conversation. "Because a lot of my students fail."

The rest of dinner was transferred to the table in blessed silence, only broken by the sounds of movement. He found the bottle of wine left chilling in the fridge and opened it to pour a glass for each of them.

"Mom and Dad never called me today." God, that sounded whiny. He took a sip of the chardonnay. "Second birthday in a row now."

Eliza smoothed her napkin in her lap, her eyes downcast to avoid looking at him. "Did you call on Mother's Day?"

Annoyance prickled at Jackson. "I was busy. I sent a card and a text message. Same as I do on birthdays."

"We all know you're busy, but…" Eliza trailed off, spreading her hands helplessly. "You've got a lot of vacation time you don't spend. Maybe if you spent some of it seeing them, it'd help."

He wondered if Eliza realized he hadn't used any of his vacation time in years. The thought of voluntarily walking away from work for any length of time felt strange. And, that was, when he thought about it, why his parents' lack of interest bothered him so much. Aside from a few friends and his sister, he didn't have any interactions outside of the hospital. In a sad way, he relied on his absentee parents to compensate for that.

"You should visit them," Eliza pressed.

"I'll think about it."

Thinking about it was probably as far as he'd ever get. He'd withdrawn so well from the world after Amy died that the ability to reach out and reconnect had shriveled up like atrophied muscle. Chris and Eliza's enduring patience made it easy, but with everyone else—his parents included—he just found it too painful to try. Rebuilding relationships after years had gone by sure as hell wasn't as easy as climbing back on a bicycle.

Chris cleared his throat to break the awkward silence. "So. What's the new intern like, then? Is she good?"

The change of subject was welcome, even if it brought him back onto Morales. "She's smart, very passionate. I worry she might be a little too emotionally involved, though. She teared up on a patient and that's just...difficult for everyone."

"You sound like you admire her, at least," Chris offered.

"She probably has the makings for a good surgeon, but almost as soon as we met we were arguing. It's like throwing dynamite into a fire, the way we clash."

"Is she hot?"

"Not funny, Chris," Eliza said.

"It's a valid question, if they're setting each other off like that."

Jackson shook his head with a sigh. "You know I shouldn't even look at an intern that way. I've had enough doomed romance for a lifetime."

"An intern isn't the same as…" A dark look from Jackson cut Chris off before he said anything more.

No, an intern wasn't the same as a dead girlfriend. Unlike Amy Elsevier, pursuing Darla would be more likely to end in one of them being transferred than grieving. Darla and Amy had other things in common, though. Anxiety, vulnerability, whatever it was that gave Jackson that need to rescue and fix. He knew from experience it was a terrible motive for a relationship.

And Morales was unquestionably hot. Her dark curls would have looked far more tempting if they'd been left loose, but her ponytail just served to draw more attention to her exquisite features. Her glasses made her otherwise girlish face seem more serious, the frames accentuating just how large and dark her eyes were. He'd always been able to appreciate women of a variety of body types, but there was something special about a petite, curvy woman—and Morales had curves to spare. She was absolutely everything that pushed his buttons, and yet...

"It doesn't matter what she looks like. I need to be professional with female colleagues."

"God, you sound like an ethics textbook," Chris said. "So keep it professional and focus on her strengths. It's easier to learn through positive reinforcement than anything else."

"That's not something I need advice on from you. You've never mentored anyone," Jackson said.

"I've trained more than my fair share of horses. People are easier because they're smarter."

Jackson had to laugh. "You're so full of shit."

"It worked on your sister, didn't it?"

"Chris!" Eliza reached over to swat Chris playfully, and he caught her hand. He pulled her closer by that hand to kiss her and Jackson had to look away, even as he felt a little surge of pride at having successfully gotten them together.

"I'm not going to treat her like a horse."

"Your loss. I'm telling you, all the animal behavior studies are clear on this. Positive reinforcement is the best way to teach someone to learn complex behaviors."

"I can't imagine anything more insulting than treating her like a lab animal."

"So you think she prefers fighting with you?" Chris countered.

"That's not what I said. There's a lot of room between training somebody like a horse and arguing with them."

"Then what are you going to do?"

"I'll be nice, but not like she's an animal. Jesus."

"We're all animals. Some of us are just a little more at peace with that than others."

"We're doctors."

"As entertainingly stupid as I find this conversation, could the two of you give it a rest?" Eliza held up her wine glass meaningfully

Jackson raised his own glass to toast to that. "Gladly."

Chapter Four

The apartment building had stucco walls on the outside and brightly colored Spanish tiles on the roof, like hundreds of others built in the area during the '90s. The first time Darla had seen them, she thought they looked charming and unique in comparison to the buildings in Chicago. But after seeing the exact same design over and over again, some of the charm had started to wear thin.

Though there was that sameness to construction, her roommate Brandon had fallen in love with this specific neighborhood. Their building was eight minutes by car from the hospital, halfway between the Smith Center for the Performing Arts and the Gay and Lesbian Community Center. Holidays and parties in the building were always entertaining with the number of residents who worked in theater. Brandon's dating life stayed pretty active too.

Brandon stopped his car under the parking lot awning. "Hey, you survived a whole day with DeMatteo. That's got to count for something."

"Pretty sure it doesn't."

Survival had never been in question. She had just wished the earth would swallow her whole a couple of times. Things had turned around by the end of the shift, though none of that could wipe out her earlier fumbles.

"Maybe next time you could take one of your pills. This is what they're for, right?"

"In theory." She drew the words out slowly, regretting not for the first time that Brandon knew about her condition. Advice from well-meaning people about things they had never experienced felt old the first time it happened. Her doctor had told her to take the beta-blockers an hour before anything particularly anxiety-inducing, to help keep her heart rate steady. They worked wonderfully for warding off the migraines or symptoms from her mitral valve prolapse, but they had their drawbacks. "Except they might also make me all sluggish and forgetful, so I'm worried about taking them at work."

"It's not like DeMatteo has that great of a memory anyway. Every time I had to do rounds with him, he forgot my name. Maybe since you messed up, you could convince him you're a different intern."

"Great. So even when I do well, he might not remember who I am?"

Brandon's phone started ringing. She glanced back to see him wander away in the parking lot as he answered it, likely looking for some measure of privacy. That was easy enough to give him, at least.

She reached the exterior staircase at the same time as her neighbors from across the hall. The two women lived together with a little girl of about five—a family, Darla assumed. One of the mothers was close to six feet in her heels, her body thin and sinewy. The other was shorter, with a softer figure closer to Darla's. Both of the mothers dressed nicely, though the little girl had something sticky and sweet smeared all over her face as she munched away at a cookie. Darla gave the family a quick smile before she started to follow them up the stairs.

"Mommy, I feel funny," the little girl said.

"You probably just had too much sugar at the party. We'll get you in a bath and into bed and it'll be fine," said the short woman holding her hand.

"But I can't..." The little girl trailed off, her words sounding strangely slurred for a kindergartner.

Darla looked closer at the girl. It was difficult to notice at first, but once she paid attention the faint wheezing from the girl was unmistakable. Her face looked ever so slightly fuller than usual as well. Swelling, most likely. "Does your daughter have any allergies?

"Excuse me?" The second woman shot Darla an offended look. "How is that any of your business?"

"Because she looks like she's having an anaphylactic reaction."

Both of the mothers turned to their daughter. The tall one dropped to one knee to look into the little girl's face, cupping her cheeks in her hands. "Susie? Susie, are you okay?"

The wheezing only grew worse as the little girl's eyes went wide with panic. Instead of responding, she tried to flail free of her mother's grasp. The shorter mother caught her before she could fall down the stairs, but both women looked nearly as panicked as their child.

Things would only get worse if she didn't step in.

Darla touched the back of the shorter woman's hand. "Do you have an EpiPen for her?"

"No! She had a bad reaction to a bee sting once, but we've never had anything like this happen before."

A bee sting. That could explain things. "Can I take that?" She took the cookie from the little girl to drop it into her pocket, then refocused on the parents. "Benadryl?"

"Inside." The taller woman raced up the stairs to unlock the apartment door. "It's all in our bathroom."

"May I?" Darla scooped Susie from the shorter woman, then followed the taller one up the stairs and into the apartment.

Her heart pounded, the now-familiar rush of adrenaline focusing her attention on reaching the bathroom and assessing the severity of the girl's reaction. Darla was so keyed up, every detail barraged her. The scent of potpourri, framed posters of Vegas stage shows on the walls of the living room, a Doc McStuffins doll left on the floor that nearly tripped her, the weight and measured breathing of the child gasping in her arms.

She shoved into the bathroom, accepting the bottle of Benadryl and setting the child to sit atop the countertop. "I need you to drink this, Susie."

The little girl's first attempt to swallow the antihistamine through her swollen throat tripped her gag reflex. Darla wrapped her arms around the little girl to soothe her and stroke her hair as she vomited, listening all the while to be sure her breathing passages were clear. A small plastic cup sat on the edge of the sink. Darla stretched to fill it without abandoning Susie entirely.

"Here. Let's rinse your mouth out really good, okay?" Honestly, Darla was thrilled the girl vomited. At least that would lessen the amount of allergen in her body, causing the anaphylaxis. She watched closely as the girl sipped and then spit the water back into the toilet. The stench of stomach acid mixed with baked goods filled the bathroom, which was already feeling too full with three adults crowded into it.

"Now let's try this again. It'll help you." Part of her worried the little girl's throat was too inflamed to swallow at all and they'd have to take her to the hospital immediately, but despite a little dribbling over her chin it seemed to go down.

Several tense minutes passed with no sound save Susie's wheezing until finally it subsided.

Darla disentangled herself and hit the handle on the toilet on her way out of the bathroom to make room for the parents to fuss over their daughter. The cookie was plastered with lint when she took it out of her pocket, but still clean enough that she could make a few educated guesses at the ingredients.

"She's okay with nuts?"

"She has a PB&J almost every day. It's never been a problem," the shorter mother said.

Darla sniffed at the cookie and nodded to herself, suspicion confirmed. "It's probably the honey that set her off, then."

The taller mother turned away from her daughter to give Darla an exasperated look. "How does honey make someone's mouth swell up?"

"Filtered, pasteurized honey is pretty inert and safe, but

if it's improperly handled or raw it can contain bee venom. It's usually only a problem in kids with bee sting allergies."

The shorter mother's mouth pursed into an outraged circle. "Oh my God. Bruce's stupid hippie food! He said those were 'raw' cookies."

"I'd just watch her around honey if you don't know it was filtered. It really shouldn't be a big concern most of the time. For tonight, you should get her in to see someone. Even with her symptoms subsiding, it's still in her system."

"Are you a doctor?" asked the taller mother.

It was a reasonable question, but it filled Darla with a warm glow all the same. "Still an intern. In a couple months, I'll be able to practice on my own, but not yet."

"Well, you saved our daughter and that's good enough for me."

"I didn't do anything you couldn't have done your-selves." The panic of the girl's parents more than anything else had been the problem. No one could blame them for responding emotionally to their child gasping for breath, but it wasn't the best frame of mind for decision making. Think-ing about it that way put her day into a new perspective. Jackson's admonishments to be less emotional had seemed arbitrary at the time.

"You *saved* her." The way the taller woman said it made it clear no counterarguments would be accepted. "My name's Rachel and this is my wife Nikki."

Now that the emergency was over, Darla could really take note of her neighbors beyond parental panic. Rachel's height wasn't quite as dramatic as it had looked at first glance. Instead, it was helped along by a precarious pair of heels and her dark curls puffed up around her face. Her makeup was flawlessly understated, highlighting her high cheekbones and full lips without ever taking center stage. Nikki was just as short and full-bodied as she'd looked at first glance, but what Darla had taken for braids before were tiny, neatly formed dreadlocks. A small gold nose ring complimented the deep brown of Nikki's skin. They were the sort of casually gorgeous women who'd always made Darla feel insecure, but there was no judgment as they looked at her. Just gratitude.

"I'm Darla. It's nice to meet you." She winced. "I mean, not that the situation is nice, but it's just…you seem nice."

Nikki laughed and that seemed to break the remaining tension. "If there's anything we can ever do for you, please let us know."

Her skin prickled with the heat of a blush. "That's not necessary. I really didn't do much."

Nikki gave her a sardonic look, then turned back into the bathroom to pick Susie up and start washing her face. "If you tell people you didn't do much, they'll eventually start believing you. You did a good thing, Darla. Own it."

A small smile tugged at the corners of her mouth. "Okay. Thank you, but I don't expect anything for helping."

"Well, I'm a hairdresser and Rachel does makeup. You ever have a hot date, you come knock on our door, all right?"

Darla laughed at the thought. The last time she'd been on a date had been back in Chicago, before she started her internship. Finding the time to meet someone and feel sexy enough to try flirting when she spent nearly every waking moment in frumpy scrubs was next to impossible. "I don't think that's very likely, but I'll remember. Keep an eye on your little girl, okay? Keep an EpiPen on hand. Just in case."

"We'll take her in to Quick Care." Rachel led her to the door, then patted her on the arm. "Have a good night."

Her feet felt a bit lighter on the walk across the hall, her head a little higher than usual. It really hadn't been anything spectacular she'd done, no matter what they said, but it had helped. *She* had helped.

Brandon stopped at the top of the stairs and eyed her, then glanced over toward the neighbors' door as Rachel shut it. "What the hell were you doing in there?"

The weight of the world came back almost immediately, her shoulders slumping. "Their daughter was having an allergic reaction, and I helped her. It's no big deal."

"Oh." He was quiet for a moment, then gave her two thumbs up. "Awesome. Anyway, any more thoughts about working with Dr. Ice?"

"DeMatteo was very...professional." She unlocked the apartment door to let them both in. It seemed to be the best word to use to describe him, rather than falling back on all of the "cold" descriptions she'd heard interns use before. They didn't seem exactly right to her. He was distant, but there wasn't anything cold about him. That might be a first impression, but after seeing him deal with those seriously injured construction workers, she knew he wasn't nearly as unaffected as he appeared to be. He could be intimidating, though.

DeMatteo was easily four or five inches taller than Brandon, who was fairly short and slim for a man. Unlike DeMatteo's naturally golden skin tone, her roommate was so pale he'd turn bright red after just a few minutes in the sun. The fact that Brandon kept his hair bleached blond and buzzed close to his scalp further robbed him of any hint of color. The bleached-out look made for a striking combination that granted him more presence than his slight build and height might have otherwise given.

"He probably hates me, but at least he isn't dropping me from his service. I don't think, anyway," Darla went on.

Brandon made a noncommittal sound and brushed past her into the kitchen. "That was Heath on the phone, and he had some juicy gossip. Apparently Dr. Ice had a girlfriend a long time ago and she killed herself. They say that's why he's such an asshole."

Hospital gossip was rarely accurate, but maybe a kernel of truth was hidden under it all. DeMatteo wouldn't be the first person to lose a loved one, and there had to be something more to him pushing people away while clearly unhappy that his parents weren't calling him. Punishing himself like that couldn't have come from nowhere. "He doesn't seem like the type to let personal problems interfere with work, though."

"People can surprise you."

Chapter Five

Darla cradled her phone as she set her lunch tray down across from Brandon and her friend Maggie, another first year resident. "Hi, Mama. What's going on?"

"Just checking in. How're things in trauma medicine?" Anita Morales asked with brittle cheerfulness.

"Uh, okay?" Darla swallowed hard, hoping she wouldn't have to go into any sort of detail. "Doing my best. I'm not sure that's enough some days."

"It is. They're lucky to have you, and Mt. Sinai Hospital will be lucky to get you, too." The words had more force to them than seemed entirely warranted, but this was typical. At some point her mother had decided to bulldoze her way through Darla's anxiety with bluster and unrealistic expectations. "Try not to worry so much, *niña*. You've been so miserable out there, but it'll be better once you're home."

Her mother was right, at least as far as her unhappiness went. Going to Las Vegas had been an adventure all its own, but that hadn't shaken the sense of deep dissatisfaction that settled over her during her first year as a surgical resident. Would returning to Chicago fix it? She wasn't sure, but there weren't any other possible solutions she could see.

"I hope so. I've got to eat before my next shift," Darla said.

"All right, honey. With the time difference it might be too late for me to call back before you're done, but send me an email. I hate not hearing from you for days at a time."

"I will."

"And remember, no matter how bad things get I'm going to be there to help you study for your Step Three exam in a couple weeks."

The reminder made her wince. The visit was welcome, but the test would finally allow her to obtain a medical license. No amount of preparation could entirely shake her nervousness over it. "Thanks, Mama."

After she'd hung up Maggie reached across the table to give Darla her cupcake from Mag's weekly bakery visit. The mounds of white frosting included, the cupcake was about four inches tall. Eating them more than once a week might have required a death wish. "What did your mom want?"

"Usual mom stuff. Do you want in on the Step Three prep when she gets here?"

Brandon shifted in his chair to pull out his own phone. "Definitely. I heard the more somebody specializes the worse they do on it, though. Is your mom going to be that helpful?"

"She's always been a help to me before." Darla poked at her potato salad with her fork. "You're not opening that flashcard app, are you?"

"C'mon. We're all together. It's the perfect time."

Maggie groaned with a shake of her head. "No, I don't want to think about cysts and parasites. I want to eat."

"There've been a lot of studies that suggest giving people downtime to relax and absorb information is better than constantly drilling them," Darla said.

"Funny how no residency program ever heard of those studies." Brandon dropped his phone and resumed picking at his food. "So Maggie and I were talking about her taking over your old room when you leave."

The potato salad felt like gravel going down her throat, settling heavily in her stomach. "I don't know if I'm even going to be accepted back in Chicago."

"We know, but Brandon had to make plans for how to pay the rent when you're gone and with my roommate bailing on me it seemed like a good solution."

"That makes sense." Everyone moving on without her was a worse lunchtime conversation than cysts and parasites. She looked around, trying to think of something else to talk about and save herself the stress of dwelling on yet another cross-country move. Her eye fell on Jackson DeMatteo, sitting by himself and reading on his phone while he ate. His thick, dark hair was slightly tousled, probably from having been shoved under a surgical cap, but it made her wonder if it looked the same when he first woke up. "I hope my next shift with him is easier."

Maggie turned to follow Darla's eye. "You should go talk to him."

"Me talking to him is what made everything go wrong in the first place."

"Yeah, but you can overcome that."

"I can overcome calling him ignorant and being thrown out of his OR?"

"You can." Maggie jabbed her fork in Darla's direction. "You're not nervous with us, because you're in your comfort zone with your friends. Go expand your comfort zone. Get to know him, relax, and show him what a badass you are."

Darla laughed self-deprecatingly. "I'm not a badass."

"You're not going to be one with that kind of attitude."

Darla drummed her nails on the edge of the table, fighting against that rising tide of agitation she knew too well. Tests and learning things were easy and it had never stopped her there, but people were different. At least new people were. Was Maggie right that she just needed to get to know him and it'd disappear? "Brandon, what do you think?"

Brandon shrugged. "I'm sorry, is this a life or death question? Go network. It's only a big deal if you make it into one."

Maggie beamed and threw an arm around Brandon's shoulders. "We've got ourselves a future motivational speaker here."

Someone else taking a seat at his table didn't tug Jackson's attention away from the article he was reading. The hospital cafeteria wasn't particularly crowded, but if someone needed the other chair at his table he wasn't about to protest. It was the giant cupcake on the edge of his field of vision that finally had him lowering his phone.

Morales sat across from him, though she didn't look particularly pleased. Her posture was stiff, her muscles held tense.

"Is something wrong?"

"No. I thought you might like company."

His eyes slid up and down over what he could see of her. The square cut of the scrubs hadn't been designed with full curves like hers in mind, and she'd obviously taken a larger size to accommodate that, but there was no hiding the lush body beneath. As near as he could tell, she wasn't wearing any makeup and her hair was once again pulled into a tight ponytail, but a few curls had escaped this time to make a fuzzy, black halo around her face. Before he could stop himself he wondered how her hair would look let down, preferably spread out over a pillow.

"Sure, I wouldn't mind some. I'd just been reading up on those hormonal effects on trauma recovery. It actually looks pretty promising." He offered a smile, watching and hoping she might start to relax.

"It does?" Some of the tension visibly left her, but it was replaced with a look of surprise. "After what you said, I thought…"

"Promising doesn't mean it's something we can actually use. It takes years of data and approval before a new treatment can be implemented. And that's a good thing, because it helps protect our patients from long-term side-effects."

Her brows raised slightly, and there was the start of a shy smile curling up one corner of her full lips. "You really thought I didn't know that? Were you worried I was going to start jabbing patients with estrogen?"

Jackson laughed in spite of himself, dragging a hand through his hair. "Probably not, but I hear people talk about new therapies and treatments and usually they're not being as cautious about it as they should be."

"I like research. Why would I want people to skip it entirely?" Her voice had a hint of teasing in it.

"I don't know. You seemed so gung-ho, and I've had a few residents who got cocky that they had all the answers before."

Her smile fully blossomed, her dark brown eyes twinkling like the night sky. For a moment, he was floored by the full force of it. There was something wrong with a woman having a smile like that and looking worried all the time.

"So you've got to crush our spirits?" she asked.

"I like to think of it more like keeping you grounded."

"And who keeps you grounded when you think you've got all the answers?"

"I don't think that."

She reached across the table to tap his phone tightly with one finger. "You didn't think this was a great idea when I first told you about it. You were wrong."

He leaned back in his chair with a roll of his eyes. "Then I guess you can be the one to keep me grounded."

"I can live with that."

He nodded toward the cupcake on her tray. "Where'd you get that? Not from the cafeteria. I would've noticed the stampede if they had anything like those."

"My friend Maggie makes a weekly bakery run for a bunch of people here. You can get in on it if you want." Darla looked down at her cupcake for a moment with a thoughtful expression, then picked up her fork to break off a piece of the cake with a healthy dollop of the frosting on top. She held the fork out to him. "No stampede necessary."

It was a cupcake, he reminded himself. There wasn't

anything erotically charged about baked goods, no matter what strange temptations he was suffering from. Still, his imagination filled with visions of sucking frosting off of her delicate fingertips. He took the fork from her and tried to ignore the electric charge he felt from his hand brushing hers.

Instead of the plain yellow cake he'd expected, it was sponge cake that had been soaked in something sweet, but with a light, simple taste of its own. At least he could recognize the frosting as whipped mascarpone with little caramel shavings in it.

"I have no idea what that is, but it's delicious."

Her laugh was full of skepticism. "Really? You've never had *tres leches* cake?"

"Not that I can remember. I've had similar desserts with soaked cake, but they're usually stronger flavored."

"You need to get out more. The cupcake's a little different from how I'm used to it, though." She took a bite of it for herself, then gestured to him. "You're welcome to share."

Eating off his own fork wasn't quite as decadent as sharing hers, but the cake was a welcome consolation. They were halfway through the giant cupcake before he remembered they both had an actual lunch to eat rather than just dessert.

He switched back to his lunch to get something other than empty calories before he was full and noticed Dick Mevlyn with a nurse just behind Darla's left shoulder. The annoyance on his face must have shown because she turned in her chair to look.

"What's wrong?"

"Just this guy who gets on my nerves." He shook his head with a sigh. "He's a fine surgeon, but a lazy instructor at the medical school, and he's always sucking up to everyone else at the hospital."

Darla went still, her eyes taking on a concerned expression. "Isn't that just networking?"

"I guess some of it is." Jackson was sure it would help his own career to do more of that, but Mevlyn just made it seem so *sleazy*. "Some of it's something else. Like he always starts flirting with women he might be able to use somehow."

She pursed her lips in a frown. "I thought that went against the fraternization policy."

"No, because he usually doesn't progress to actually dating them as near as I can tell. He doesn't do it with anyone that he directly supervises or who supervises him either. If I wanted to go around flirting with nurses and residents I don't work with, that'd be fine, but you and I couldn't have a relationship." After the words were out, he felt a sinking sensation in his stomach. Why had he used that example? It was true, but it wasn't really appropriate to point out, was it? Though maybe more appropriate than thinking about sucking frosting off of her fingers.

"Oh." Darla's face was slowly turning red before she ducked her head to try to avoid his eyes. "I guess that makes sense."

"I mean, as an example. If a resident and the attending they worked under started a relationship, the resident would have to be transferred," he explained. "Just for everyone's own good, so there couldn't be a question of harassment or favoritism."

It was a sensible policy, he knew. But for once he found himself just a bit disappointed it existed.

Chapter Six

The fact that interns were constantly being cycled through the services of other doctors had always been a blessing in the past. Days or weeks could go by without crossing paths with a specific intern, giving time for hurt feelings over little slights to be forgotten. Days without working with Morales again hadn't been the welcome relief Jackson wanted, though. Partly because her insatiable quest for knowledge made him feel like he was actually doing what he was meant to be doing, and partly because every day she hadn't been in his rotation had been a day he'd spent thinking about her, wondering how she fared with her other rounds, while he surreptitiously glanced up and down the halls for a glimpse of her gorgeous hair and sweet smile.

"Did you know turmeric can kill oral cancer cells?"

Jackson stopped stirring the cream into his coffee. Days without working with her hadn't been a relief, but somehow five minutes in her presence was already overwhelming. Not in an annoying kind of way, but more in the sense that he couldn't ignore the stirrings of attraction that he felt in response to her nearness. Her penchant for spouting random facts and barraging him with studies and data? Yeah. He rather liked anticipating what she'd say next. It kept him on his toes. Case in point, wherever she was going with turmeric.

"What?"

She hadn't had any coffee, at least not as near as he could tell. She was just that chipper once her anxiety melted away, practically bouncing on her heels in pleasure over her latest factoid. It wasn't natural. Although it was kind of cute.

"There's a chemical in turmeric," she said, "called curcumin, and it's been found to kill oral cancer cells. It's also as effective at treating gingivitis as medicated mouthwash."

He sipped his coffee, mulling that over. "Turmeric. Like the herb?"

"Yeah, it's what makes curry powder yellow. Isn't that so cool?"

Already he could feel himself being pulled along with her enthusiasm, down roads he couldn't go. Not if he wanted to keep his distance. "It sounds like some sort of alterna-health bullshit, frankly." As soon as he saw the disappointment in her big brown eyes he regretted his words. He spoke again in a gentler tone. "Where did you get that?"

She gave a brief shrug. "There were studies."

"How many?"

"I…a lot."

He marveled that someone could be so knowledgeable and optimistic about every new treatment at the same time. That her enthusiasm for medicine hadn't been crushed by the world when she was clearly so sensitive had to count for something.

Halfway through his coffee, a page came through. He swallowed down as much as he could, then took Morales with him to the ambulance bay. The EMTs arrived moments after they walked through the doors and took a screaming little boy out on the gurney. He cast a look in Darla's direction, hoping she wouldn't start crying and make things worse.

"Seven year old white male, fell off the back of a personal watercraft on Lake Mead and hit in the abdomen by the exhaust," an EMT said as they wheeled him in.

It wasn't the first personal watercraft accident he'd dealt with, but it was also far from the worst and for that he was grateful. The force of water and air had left his entire abdomen bruised, but the skin was intact. That was certainly better than alternatives he'd seen, where skin was torn and organs were completely detached.

Morales took the little boy's hand, patting the back of it. "Shh. Stay calm. It's going to hurt more if you cry. Just breathe with me, all right? We're going to get you fixed up."

Whatever had happened to improve her bedside manner since the last time he'd worked with her, he approved. Soon the screaming boy settled as he focused on matching his breathing with Darla's.

Further examination found the boy's stomach hard to the touch, sending a chill down Jackson's spine. Not the worst he'd seen, but far from the best. "Page Dr. White and get me an OR stat. This internal bleeding can't wait."

"What's happening? What are you doing?" The little boy started to thrash in a panic, but barely managed to move before he screamed in pain again.

Darla squeezed his hand and braced her other hand on

his shoulder to push him back down. "Dr. DeMatteo's going to help you. Just hold still. Breathe with me again."

As they wheeled him to the OR, Jackson kept waiting for the other shoe to drop with Darla. Focusing on his patient was priority, but that didn't stop him from looking at her, watching for some trembling of her hands or catch in her voice. In contrast, her own attention never wavered from the little boy until she had to leave him to prep for surgery.

Another doctor pushed her way in through the operating room doors and cast a quick, assessing glance over the little boy. Dr. Nancy White was a tall, slender woman with silver streaks through her blond hair, though that hair was currently covered. Her pale blue eyes narrowed over her face mask. "What do we have here?"

Jackson nodded to Darla. "Morales, were you paying attention?"

"Oh. Um." She looked nonplussed by this and Jackson felt a spark of annoyance. Was this when she'd fall apart? "Seven year old male suffering blunt force trauma to the abdomen with internal bleeding." Her description went on for a moment. The words were a little halting, and he could see the stiffness in her shoulders as she spoke, but all the details were there.

Jackson gave her a nod of approval. "Good."

"Have you ever scrubbed into surgery before?" Nancy asked as they began.

"Five times."

The answer was out almost before Nancy finished her question and Jackson had to grin at the promptness. She was still at the point when each individual surgery stood out in her mind. He remembered those days well. The fact that they were still prominent in his memory made their importance clear. What she learned now would have more of a lasting effect than all the lessons to follow.

Despite the poor impression she'd given their first day together, her hands were steady as they worked on the patient. There was a rhythm to surgery when things went well. Like a dance, each movement was choreographed. The fewer complications, the fewer deviations from that plan and rhythm. It took time to learn the rhythm and be able to follow it without getting in anyone's way, but Darla never faltered. Her lack of experience was more than made up for by her attentiveness and what seemed to be an ability to anticipate his next move. McGaffey had spotted a natural talent under all those nerves.

"You ever thought about a specialty track in PEDS?" Nancy's admiring tone sent a possessive shock through Jackson. Just getting her good enough for Singh's approval and not driving her off had seemed difficult enough before. Other doctors trying to scalp her from the trauma department would make his Herculean task next to impossible.

Darla shook her head. "Oh, no. I'm going into trauma. It's what I've always wanted."

The tension drained from Jackson's body, leaving him light and empty. Regardless of whatever talents Nancy saw, Darla's sights were set on one thing and one thing only. That it perfectly coincided with what he needed was a boon.

"Kids get trauma, too." Nancy gave a meaningful nod down toward the boy on the surgery table. "They're not just little adults, either. It's a whole other challenge to work on them."

"I know and I'd like to, but..." Darla trailed off, her

brows knitted together and her eyes cast to the side to avoid looking at either one of them.

Her reaction intrigued him. Some sort of conflict was clearly at play, but why? And, more importantly, was it something that would come back to bite him in the end?

He cleared his throat. "Morales, would you like to close up?"

Even with half her face hidden, the sudden light in her eyes was apparent. "Thank you, Dr. DeMatteo."

He watched to verify she knew what she was doing, finding himself pleasantly surprised again. Whatever her faults, a lack of knowledge and skill weren't among them. Though she was fairly slow at the work, she did it methodically and well. Speed would come with time.

When the surgery was done and Jackson stepped out with Nancy, the pediatric surgeon stopped him. "I can't believe that's the intern you were complaining about."

Had he said anything about her to anyone? Other than Singh on that first day, he'd kept most of his opinions to himself. They were too complicated when it came to Morales. "I haven't been complaining about her."

"Mevlyn said you were."

That man played dirty politics at every turn. Jackson had to hope there wouldn't be any false gossip getting back to Darla.

"It was a bad first impression." Not that she had been terrible, he had to admit, but the fact that she'd immediately insulted him had colored his view of her negatively. He opened his mouth to try to explain that things had gotten better and the door behind them creaked shut. Rather than speak, he checked to be sure.

Darla stood there, eyes wide with hurt. Damn it.

Nancy just smiled. Maybe Melvyn wasn't the only one with an agenda. "Hey, a couple of our volunteers for the gala have backed out. Would you be interested, Morales?"

Darla's shoulders settled, her features smoothing out, but there was still something guarded in her voice when she spoke. "A gala? What for?"

Jackson considered Nancy's smile once again. Was he being paranoid or was she really out to steal his intern? "It's a big fund-raising event for the children's hospital and the medical school. We usually get a bunch of interns to volunteer and chat up the donors and tell them how vital their money is," he said. "It's probably not something you'd be interested in."

Instead of agreeing with him and dismissing Nancy's offer, Darla looked offended. "Why wouldn't I? That sounds fun."

Fun for people who liked that sort of thing, maybe. Though she'd done better since her panic that first day, he still couldn't imagine Darla enjoying the fundraiser much. He rarely did. "It can be, but it's pretty...stuffy. Especially for the interns. You're not really doing much but smiling and nodding."

Her fists settled on her hips, chin raising defiantly. It was that same spark he'd seen in her when she'd called him ignorant—the sort of fire that would serve a surgeon well—but he wondered when her vulnerable side would win out. "I can smile and nod."

"And do you want to do that for hours on end? In heels?"

Her eyes narrowed, and she straightened her spine, gaining an inch or so in height. "I can wear heels."

Shit. This was rapidly spiraling out of control. He raised his hands to ward off any more defensive responses from her. "I didn't mean you can't wear heels. I just meant it doesn't seem like the sort of thing you'd be into."

She answered that with a tilt of her head and a cocked brow. "How the hell do you know what I'd be into?"

Nancy clapped her hands together and smiled brightly. "Great! It's settled. I look forward to seeing you there, Morales."

Jackson glared at Nancy's back as she walked away, then turned back to Darla. Her soft bronze skin had gone a shade paler, her lips pressed so tightly together they'd formed a flat line. He felt a touch smug at that, because of course he'd been right.

"And do you want to go to the gala?"

"God no!"

He laughed. "Can't resist a challenge?"

She wrinkled her nose, shaking my head. "It's not that. I just hate being told what I should or shouldn't do."

"Problems with authority? I never would have guessed you were such a rebel," he teased. "You can go track her down and tell her that, if you want. Or you can just go."

Instead of an immediate answer, she looked thoughtful. He did his best not to stare when her tongue darted out to wet her bottom lip. "I don't think my roommate volunteered, and we have to share a car. Where's the gala?"

"I can drive you." What the hell was he doing? The words were out before he'd thought it through. It was the decent thing to offer, but he was already picturing the difficulty of being in a car with her alone. "It's at a golf course outside of town, and it's black tie."

"Oh." Worry crossed her face like a cloud in front of the sun.

Memories of his own limited wardrobe as an intern surfaced. He'd had one suit for years, but it looked good on him. Fashion wasn't nearly as forgiving for women. "Can you do formal?"

"Yes, yes, of course I can." The words came out quickly, jumbling together. Her eyes flicked to the side to avoid his gaze. "I don't walk around in scrubs and ponytails on my days off, you know."

"Nothing wrong with scrubs and ponytails." The way she dressed was practical, which was better than some other interns he'd worked with who left long hair down until he yelled at them. Even better than practical, she could fill out her scrubs the way some women filled out evening gowns. Her body looked soft and inviting, in need of exploration. This time he was the one who looked away to get his thoughts back under control. "Give me your address, and I'll pick you up around a quarter past four on Friday. It's a bit of a drive."

Once she gave him her address and number, she went off to check on his patients. He watched after her, too many thoughts fighting against one another. There was potential to her, that much was clear, but what she'd said during surgery nagged at him. If trauma wasn't her true passion, what was going to happen further down the road?

Chapter Seven

By the time Darla found DeMatteo to give him his updates, he was settled in at the table in the center of the attending lounge and looked to be busy grading papers. Some of his work from the medical school, she assumed. The closest thing to downtime she'd seen him take so far was when he was drinking his coffee. His constant, intense focus was impressive, but she wondered when he ever let himself relax.

"Mr. Miller in room two-forty-three wanted to know how active he can be when he gets home, and I wasn't sure how to answer," she said.

DeMatteo accepted the tablet from her to check Mr. Miller's chart and leaned back from the laptop. "The body builder? He can't train for at least a month after that amount of blood loss. I'd say anything more than ten minutes of walking a day would be useless stress until then."

Trying to imagine how the huge and impatient man

would react to that news made her shudder. "I don't look forward to telling him that."

"There are far worse things we have to tell patients." DeMatteo set the tablet down when his pager went off. He checked it with a frown. "But that'll have to wait."

She followed him out, expecting him to head for the ambulance bay, but instead he went for the elevator. Inside, he hit the button for the seventh floor.

"Why are we going to obstetrics?" she asked.

"They sent me an emergency page for one of their ORs. Do you know why they'd page a trauma surgeon?"

That was an easy question, at least. "Any surgical intervention will create a degree of trauma, while both cesarean sections and vaginal birth can lead to hemorrhage."

"You're going to spend a lot more time talking to patients and their families than writing essays. Give me the Twitter version."

She bit her lip. What kind of answer did he want? "They page you when something's gone wrong."

"That's right." There was a trace of a smile on his lips when he met her eyes, but he didn't look terribly happy. "Something's gone wrong."

It would be so easy to reach out and touch him. A hand on the arm in solidarity, or even cupping his cheek. Seeing his worry before he'd stepped into the operating room made everything nurturing in her want to reassure him, but nothing she could think of seemed appropriate. Badass surgeons didn't need comfort from interns, did they?

As soon as the doors opened, Jackson sprinted down the hall to the scrub room. Before she'd caught up with him he was already washing his hands.

Rather than charging forward, she hung back. "Should I scrub in?"

He shook his head, his jaw tense. "Not this time. There's already a surgical team in there, and it's an emergency situation."

Then what am I even doing here? She kept the comment to herself, though her silence did little to quell her frustration. It wasn't the first time someone had decided a situation was too serious to be used for teaching. When there was little she could do to help, the best she could do was watch. It just wasn't what she wanted.

The scrub room had a window into the operating room, letting her watch the drama unfold. She'd observed a cesarean section before and even without them paging DeMatteo, she could have guessed that things had gone badly. The baby was whisked out of the room while the staff did what they could to control the mother's bleeding. As soon as Jackson stepped into the OR, she could see him taking charge. She could imagine the short, precise orders he was giving, not needing to shout like some doctors. He took command more effortlessly than that.

From the massive hemorrhaging and what she could see of the poor woman, Darla guessed it was a complication with the placenta. Accreta was when the placenta attached abnormally and had difficulty detaching. The worse complications were increta or percreta, where the placenta either grew into the uterine muscle or surrounding organs. The chances of any of the complications went up with each C-section a patient underwent.

And all of that had seemed troubling enough in the abstract, but watching it in person was so much worse. Her hands curled into fists, and she braced them on the edge of the sink as she watched, helpless to do anything but bear witness. Not wanting to stand back and do nothing was exactly why she'd wanted to become a doctor in the first place.

After nearly fifteen minutes, what had been a losing battle officially became a lost cause and they called time of death. Jackson turned away from the scene, and his haunted eyes met hers through the window.

Out in the hall she caught up with him, though this time he wasn't running anywhere for an emergency. He'd pulled off the surgical gown over his scrubs and had dropped onto a bench. He didn't look up as she approached, or when she sat next to him.

"Are you okay?"

He raised his head, one brow arched. He'd looked worried in the elevator. Now he looked thoroughly worn down. The tension was etched into his face, his shoulders tight as if they were supporting some great weight. "Me?"

"Yeah. It's not easy to lose a patient."

He frowned and reached up to pull his surgical cap off, then raked a hand through his thick brown hair. "I've lost patients before. It's nothing new."

"That doesn't make it easier, does it?"

"Probably not." He braced his back against the wall, stretching out his long, lean legs. "There's always that guilt."

"You did the best you could. That's nothing to feel guilty over."

"Yeah?" That urge to reach out and touch him was back again. "Then how come I still feel that way?"

That was an easy question to answer, though she knew the answer didn't always make much of a difference.

"Because sometimes we feel things that aren't real. We feel guilty when we did everything right or scared when we're safe or isolated when we have friends."

He laughed. "Which is completely unhelpful."

She smiled and reached for his hand, because she couldn't resist a comforting gesture any longer. The way his fingers slid between hers before entangling with them and squeezing made her shiver, nerve endings all at attention. It should have been a friendly touch of support, but it didn't feel that way. "Yeah, it can be. But we can always ask people we trust for input."

"So what do you think my real feelings should be?"

Did that mean he trusted her? She swallowed hard. "Sad. It's a sad thing when someone dies, and it's okay to feel that. Guilt is about trying to assign blame and act like things can be controlled, but sometimes they can't be. They're just sad." And losing that mother—it was awful. But she'd watched, assessed the situation as it unfolded, there was nothing that could've been done differently. It was tragic and it was horrible, and the shock of witnessing a woman die—it wasn't something that she'd be forgetting any time soon. But he didn't need her tears or words that would add to the misplaced guilt he was feeling.

He nodded, his thumb tracing over one of her knuckles. "Guilt feels more productive somehow. Letting it go is like admitting defeat."

"We can't always win."

"But I prefer to."

He leaned closer, drawing her attention to the afternoon stubble on his cheeks and the warm scent of his aftershave. Where his thigh rested against hers on the bench burned a line through her scrubs. She wanted to feel his stubble under her fingers and trace the contours of his full lips with them. Or, better yet, use her own lips. She couldn't, of course. Not at work, not with him.

A newborn baby cried from a delivery room down the hall. Hardly an unusual sound in a maternity ward, but enough to remind Jackson of where he was. He drew back, his hand still in hers for the moment. Anyone else and a bit of emotional support between coworkers wouldn't raise an eyebrow, but they weren't anyone else and he was feeling a lot more than just support after losing a patient.

No other coworker had ever taken his hand and asked him how he was after a bad surgery, either. Or fed him cupcakes. Or called him ignorant in front of the chief. Darla was unique.

Reluctantly, he freed his hand. The loss of that small connection felt so much bigger than it should have.

"I appreciate your concern." The words were formal, meant to push distance between them even if that was the last thing he wanted.

Darla's deep brown eyes were full of concern, carefully watching him. "Should I go answer Mr. Miller's questions on my own?"

"No, I'll come with you." The finer points of keeping a body builder from pushing himself too hard were better handled by an experienced surgeon. He got up from the bench to go with her. Maybe explaining himself a little to Darla would help. Not about Amy, not at work, but some of the difficulty of opening up again. He hadn't always been this way. And for some reason, he wanted her to know that.

"You know those busy, long shifts when you never get a chance to stop for meals?" he asked.

There was no concern in her eyes now, at least. She stared at him in confusion. "Yeah?"

"And you know how your blood sugar crashes and eventually you're so hungry even when you can finally stop to get food, you just can't make yourself eat?"

"Sure. It's like going so long without sleep that when you get to bed you have insomnia. Things can be counterintuitive when we deny a need for too long." She walked ahead of him into the elevator. "There's only one way to deal with it."

"And what's that?"

"Just start again."

He shook his head. Easier said than done, but he didn't point that out. Pushing the metaphor any further would make it all too obvious what he was really hungering for.

Chapter Eight

For some women, shopping was a way to unwind. Retail therapy helped wash their cares away and make them feel like they had regained control of some little corner of their lives. Darla Morales was not one of those women. Clothes were too long for her short legs or transformed her chest into a loaf boob or created weird bumps and rolls on her stomach. Just checking the sizes and trying to figure out what would fit her was too stressful. After spending an hour looking at dresses in the mall, she'd given up. The very next saleswoman who walked up to her and asked, "Can I help you find anything?" had been presented with a credit card and a desperate plea.

Half an hour later she had a dress, stockings, shoes, and a whole new host of problems.

That was what brought her to her neighbors' doorstep with a bag clutched in her hands and panic in her eyes.

Nikki looked her over, finely sculpted brows raising

up nearly to her hairline. "Are you okay? You look like something's wrong."

Darla took a deep breath, then expelled every bit of oxygen on her next sentence. "I have to go to a formal fundraiser for the hospital, and I'm going to look like an idiot."

"Oh." The concern Nikki had shown moments before evaporated, and she leaned against the door frame. "So when is it?"

"Tomorrow night."

Nikki pursed her lips in thought. "Well…Rachel and I can't help you tomorrow. We'll be doing hair and makeup for Cirque du Soleil, but we could help you out tonight."

From further inside the apartment, a voice called out, "Who is it, honey?"

"It's Darla. She's got some party to get ready for."

Rachel came over by the door and gestured Darla in. "Susie's just gone down for bed. Let's see what we can do."

Once Darla was inside, she set her bag down and drew the dress out. The saleswoman had assured her that the black was appropriate for a black tie event and would be flattering without being too daring. The gown was strapless with a heart-shaped bodice and a long, narrow skirt that flared slightly outward from her knees. A mermaid gown, the saleswoman had called it. Lace panels scooped in at the waist from the sides to make an hourglass shape, though to her relief her skin wasn't exposed through the lace. The panels were lined with honey gold cloth that nearly matched her skin. There had been other dresses the saleswoman had shown her, but she'd spent more time than she wanted to admit wondering what Jackson would like. Something about the classic cut of the dress paired with the tease of the lace had seemed right. When he saw it would he give her another one of those looks that made it hard to breathe?

"It's at a golf course, and I have to talk to donors. I thought I'd wear this?"

"Mm." Rachel considered the dress. "We can make that work. If I show you how to do your makeup and Nikki helps with your hair, do you think you can repeat what we show you?"

"It can't be that much harder than surgery, can it?" Even to her own ears, Darla sounded desperately hopeful.

The other two women laughed, not unkindly, and Nikki gave her a reassuring pat on the arm. "It's hard, but you only have to know how to do it for one specific person. That'll make it easier, since you won't have to figure out different hair types and things like that."

"I'll get the wine!" Rachel handed the dress back.

Darla followed Nikki into the bedroom, where she was gently but firmly pressed down into a chair in front of their vanity. That uncomfortable feeling of her own reflection staring back at her made the little hairs on the back of her neck stand up.

"Sit there and let me get a good look at your hair, okay?" Nikki pulled Darla's pony tail loose, making her wince, and then began fluffing out her hair. Once she seemed satisfied with that, she grabbed a hank of it to examine the ends. She tsked. "We're gonna have to cut a lot of this off. Are you okay with that?"

Darla reached for her hair protectively. "You have to cut it off? Why?"

"Because you've abused it to hell and back. When was the last time you deep conditioned?"

"I...is that like when you leave the conditioner on for a long time?"

The mirror reflected a pitying look in Nikki's eyes. "Didn't your mama ever teach you how to take care of this?"

"No, my mom's never been interested in stuff like that. My cousins were the ones in the family into hair care."

"And what did your cousins tell you?" She began working a comb through Darla's hair.

"You know, normal stuff. Shampoo twice, switch your shampoo every couple of weeks to keep it from building up a residue, leave your conditioner on for sixty seconds."

"And what did your cousins' hair look like?"

"Shiny, pretty."

Rachel appeared to put a glass of wine into Darla's hand. "You mean straight?"

"Um." Visions of her cousins with their sleek, straight hair that they had to fuss with to ever make it keep a curl came to mind. They'd always expressed envy for her hair and how little she had to work with it. After all, she didn't need to *add* curl, did she?

Rachel and Nikki shared a look. "You've basically got a lifetime of shitty hair care to make up for here. We're gonna cut it, we're gonna deep condition, and I'll get you set so you can keep curlers in overnight and then do some very simple styling for tomorrow, but you're gonna need a lot more lessons than this."

An entire world she'd never considered was opening up before her, leaving her lost and a little exasperated. "I need hair lessons?"

"You can do some low maintenance styles, but you'll still have to take care of it. You've got 3B hair. Do you know what that means?"

She shifted uncomfortably in the chair. "No."

"Curly hair's more fragile than straight. Every place where it's curling into one of these little corkscrews? That's a breaking point. You need to take care of it right to prevent that."

"Okay."

She downed her wine for courage, then went into the bathroom to wash her hair to Nikki's specifications. While Nikki cut and conditioned and worked whatever hair magic she had, Rachel began working on her face. That, just like her hair, turned out to be more complicated than Darla had expected. Rachel wouldn't even touch her face until her skin had been exfoliated and moisturized and then she began with shaping her brows. A tiny edge of panic began to curl around Darla's heart, making her wonder if these elaborate rituals were what *all* women did every day, and she'd been failing at her gender since puberty. A lovely thought.

Rachel smoothed base on with a sponge and tipped Darla's chin up as she blended her jawline. "Tell me how you usually do your makeup, so we stay in your comfort zone."

Darla shrank a little lower in the chair. "I hardly ever wear makeup because I feel like a clown when I do."

Nikki stopped wrapping her hair in rollers for a moment to lean around and meet her eyes with a teasing smile. "Are you sure you weren't raised by wolves?"

At her panicked look, Rachel laughed softly. "It's fine. I didn't grow my hair out or put on makeup until I was eighteen and living on my own."

Hearing that was like a balm for her nerves. She took a deep breath and relaxed on the exhale. If Rachel had learned it well enough to be a professional that late in life, she could be quasi-functional at it. "But I'll have to wear makeup for this fundraiser."

Rachel held Darla's face still and began applying eyeliner. "Yeah, so I'm going to show you how to do it light, since we don't want to do anything that makes you stop looking like you."

"Isn't not looking like me the point of a makeover?"

"No. If you wanted, I could do contouring and turn you into Eva Mendes's twin, but that's for show. What you need is confidence, and confidence comes from being you and feeling good about being you."

"I don't think that's possible."

"Then we've got a lot of work to do."

Following Rachel's steps and techniques with the makeup left her head spinning like her first day in calculus. The step by step transformation of her face was fascinating to watch, even if the view was slightly blurred without her glasses. What she'd taken for effortlessly flawless looks in so many other people was rapidly coming into her own grasp.

"This is really amazing and so much more than I expected," Darla said. "Is there anything more I can do for you for this? Do you need a babysitter some night or something?"

Nikki laughed. "If that's what you want, we'd love to take advantage, but this is the kind of thing we do for fun."

"It's true." Rachel swiped lip gloss across Darla's lower lip for a final touch, then stepped back for her to admire in the mirror. "On our date night when we can't get a sitter to go out, we'll do 'fashion montages' where we cycle through all our formal wear and dance around in here."

"You should join us sometime. I'd love to try on that

dress you just got, and I have a couple you might like. There are even a few of Rachel's dresses you might fit."

Darla cast a skeptical eye on Rachel's tall, thin frame. "Are they made out of spandex?"

Rachel turned to the side to strike a pose and grinned. "My hips are about the same size as Nikki's. Being tall makes me look narrower than I really am."

Nikki put a cap over the finished curlers in Darla's hair. "This'll help hold them in place tonight. Do you have a good bra for the fundraiser?"

Darla looked down at herself with a sigh. "I'm wearing one."

"Which is fine, but you'll need a strapless one for that gown. I think you're about my size. Let's try."

Why hadn't she thought of that when she bought the gown? She mentally cursed herself for never thinking of it, but accepted the bra to try on. It felt strange to wear a bra without the constant drag on her shoulders from the straps, and she fiddled with it for a few minutes before she felt satisfied enough to step out of the bathroom.

Nikki looked her up and down, then gently pushed back her shoulders and urged her into straightened posture. It didn't feel like much of a difference until she looked in the mirror and saw the subtle transformation. If she looked like *that* in her scrubs, sharing the bench with Jackson in the hall might have ended differently. Possibly with them being fired.

"Oh wow," she breathed. "Can I borrow this?"

"No, I told you to try it on just to taunt you. Of course!"

Darla smiled tentatively, finding it difficult now to keep her eyes off the reflection she'd wanted so badly to avoid before. "I was going to wear contact lenses to the gala. Do you think that's…still me?"

Rachel handed Darla her glasses so she could see her reflection better. "Do you feel comfortable in them?"

"Yeah, I guess."

"Then wear contacts. The point here isn't to look like anybody else but you, remember."

"But I'm…me. Shouldn't I try to look better than that?"

"You should look like the best you there is." Nikki topped off their wine glasses before sipping from her own. "Performers are okay looking like somebody else, but that's on stage. You need to be you, and if you're trying to be somebody else, that's gonna show. You're not a skinny girl with straight hair, so stop acting like you're supposed to be."

Hearing it put so baldly made Darla choke on her wine. She spluttered, eyes blinking rapidly to try to fight off watering and ruining her makeup. "After all that work, you're saying it was pointless?"

"Not skinny doesn't mean not beautiful. This is what you look like, Darla. Own it."

Rachel took the chair in front of the vanity and leaned back with her long legs crossed while she sipped her wine. "You have anyone in particular you're trying to impress at this thing?"

"I guess I need to impress everyone."

"Mmhmm. I mean someone specific. You know, a special guy. Or woman. Or some other gender variation, I don't discriminate."

Unbidden, a mental image of Jackson popped into her head. His dark brown hair and those intense green eyes that made her squirm. His full lips that frowned far too often. His deep infectious laugh that she rarely got to hear. Yes. She wanted to impress him.

"Come on." Nikki gave her a prod on the shoulder. "There's gotta be somebody."

Just trying to picture how Jackson's gaze might darken and intensify with lust made her cheeks burn in a blush. "No."

It was silly to expect anything. She knew that. Getting involved with him wasn't even an option, really. But they'd be away from work and alone for a while in his car. Who knew what could happen?

Chapter Nine

It wasn't a date. Yes, Jackson was at a woman's door and dressed in a tuxedo and was going to drive her to a place where drinking and dancing would rule the night. She would, hopefully, be a bit dressed up herself. If all went well, the evening would be pleasant. It still wasn't a date. Telling himself that did little to ease his anticipation, though.

The door opened inward and for a few seconds his brain scrambled to make sense of what he was seeing. Even in scrubs, it had been clear that Darla had a lush figure, but the gown she wore might as well have been sewn especially to hug her curves. Her shoulders were bare and looked golden and inviting in contrast to the vivid black of the dress. Lace dipped in at her waist and curled around her breasts and he had to stare for a moment to reassure himself it was only cloth he saw behind the lace and not her bare skin. Even with that in mind, he couldn't shake the places the visual sent his mind. Was the skin of her stomach and breasts the same warm tone as the cloth, or was it a shade paler from not being exposed to sunlight?

"Hi." Her voice sounded uncertain, and he forced his eyes up from the dress and her body to her face.

Her hair was down and swept to one side, the black curls brushing her shoulders looking softer and glossier than he remembered them. For the most part, her makeup was subtle enough he hardly noticed it, except for her lips. He knew that red wasn't natural, though he couldn't complain. Her lips looked full and ripe and sweet as berries. He'd always found the cliché of a woman taking off her glasses to reveal her hidden beauty to be stupid, but as he met her dark brown eyes he recognized a far more compelling side to the loss of her glasses.

It was, in a way, one step closer to being naked.

"Wow. You look…amazing."

Only when it melted away did he notice how much tension she'd been holding in her body. Her smile was one of relief, but the invitation in it made him feel a different kind of tension entirely. "Thank you. You look nice yourself."

"Are you ready to go?"

She nodded and shut the door behind her. Keeping his eyes off of her was more difficult than he'd expected while he led the way to his car. The dress and styling was all nice, but he'd known she was beautiful before. Something else had changed, something more subtle. Was there a little bit of a sway to her hips? A confidence that had been lacking before? Her shoulders were squared, her spine straight, but it didn't look stiff or affected. Whatever had done it, he approved.

At his car, he unlocked her door for her and held it open.

Instead of getting in she stared at it.

"This is your car?"

He finally managed to tear his eyes away from her to look at the car. There wasn't anything wrong with it that he could see, other than it being an older Chevrolet Impala. It ran well, which was the important part. His sister Eliza had insisted on getting the damage from her fender bender in it fixed, though he'd told her not to worry about it, so it had a fresh white paint job.

"Is there a problem with it?"

"No, it's fine." She climbed in and smoothed out her skirt. "I was just surprised. Usually I see other doctors driving Mercedes and BMWs."

"Actually, I think Jags are in fashion this year." The radio hummed to life with the engine, and he turned it back down. "But keeping to some image like that never really appealed to me. I like to stick with what works."

"Oh." She looked around the interior of the car, nodding slowly. "That seems very sensible."

Sensible. The word sounded perfectly complimentary, but it chafed. Did he really want to be seen as sensible? It was the last thing he wanted to hear from a beautiful woman, followed closely by declaring him just like a brother.

Not that it's a date, he reminded himself.

He drummed his fingers on the steering wheel, searching his mind for a new topic. Something that took the focus off of him. All he could think of was how she looked, but that wasn't appropriate to talk about, was it? It wouldn't be... sensible. *Damn it.*

"Your hair looks different. Did you cut it?"

She blinked and then her lips slowly drew up in a shy

smile. "A friend of mine did it. While yelling at me about how badly I'd treated my hair before."

He chuckled. "I thought it looked fine before, but this is…nice."

She turned in her seat to face him as much as she could without taking off her seatbelt. That teasing look in her eyes made it difficult to keep focused on the road. "Only nice?"

"I could come up with a few more adjectives for it if you want, but I'm not exactly an expert on describing hair. Nice is probably the best you're going to get."

"Then I'll take what I can get." There was a slight breathiness to her voice, like she was holding back a laugh, but it made him think of other ways he could make her breathless.

The drive to Cascata Golf Course took a little over half an hour, dragged out in part because of afternoon traffic. In a way, he found the traffic to be a blessing. It held his attention captive, making it easier to keep his eyes and thoughts off Darla beside him.

As they took the winding road to the front gates, she gasped in shock and leaned forward as if that would give her a clearer view. "This is it?"

The clubhouse was tucked up into the Black Hills of the River Mountains, surrounded by desert on all sides. Yet despite that, a man-made waterfall over four hundred feet tall came cascading down the side of the course's mountain backdrop, running off into a river that meandered through the property before passing through the club house itself. Afternoon light bathed the mission-style buildings in a golden glow, punctuated by the deep shadows created by the hills themselves.

He gave her a crooked smile, raising one brow. "Gotta

make donors feel like they're getting their money's worth. Philanthropy is nice, but expensive liquor opens wallets."

"How do they even get the water for a place like this out here?"

He shrugged. "You'd have to ask my sister. She keeps up on all the water usage and rights. She's got a couple of angry rants about this place, I imagine."

As volunteers, they were directed to the employee parking, leaving the valet lot for the donors and honored guests. He opened the car door for Darla, then offered her his hand to help her out. The touch of her fingers curling around his palm sent an unexpected jolt of awareness through his body. Her eyes widened and her lips parted slightly. Surely, she had to be feeling the same draw he was. The urge to taste her lips and feel her body against his came on him in full force. Rather than leading her to the clubhouse, he took a step closer to her and brushed one of her dark curls off her shoulder. His fingers lingered there, then trailed up the side of her neck.

Another car pulling into the lot broke the spell, reminding him of where they were and, more importantly, who they were. Jackson drew back abruptly. Darla's brows drew together in confusion, before hurt flashed in her eyes.

"Dr. White is coordinating the intern volunteers. We'd better find her." Not what he wanted to do, but certainly the wiser option. He led her inside to where Nancy was preparing the other interns, doing his best the entire way to keep his eyes off Darla. If he didn't look, he wouldn't see that disappointment again, reflecting his own desires. "I'll see you at the end of the night to drive you home."

If Darla had anything more to say, he didn't stick around

to hear it. He walked to the huge windows of the event room, which overlooked the artificial oasis of the course. There was nothing productive in staring at the landscaping, but he needed the distance it put between them.

A figure walked past his peripheral vision, then stopped. "Was that Morales?" Dick Mevlyn asked.

"Yes, it was."

He was quiet for a moment. Jackson started to hope he might have walked away until Dick leaned up against the window beside him and crossed his arms. "She looks good. I'm surprised. Did they up her medication or something?"

Jackson shook his head in disgust. "Don't do that."

The smirk Dick gave in response begged to be punched away. "It's a joke. Everybody can see what a basket case she is."

The pointed barbs were nothing new, but he was in no mood for them, particularly not when they were directed at Darla. "She's not a basket case. She's young and a little nervous. We all were once."

Dick scoffed softly. "We don't all cry at work."

The entire hospital must have heard about it. He hadn't told anyone, but other people had seen her tear up. They must have been talking. It had likely already made it back to the Chief of Trauma Medicine too. The fact that it was Dick of all people to bring it up was especially galling. Who was he to harp on an intern for being human? The man would probably pass a turnip in one of his classes as long as it had perfect attendance.

Rather than listen to Dick, he went to the bar and ordered a scotch, content that the alcohol would be worked out of his blood by the time he was behind the wheel. He leaned against the bar and faced the room, sipping the oaky single-malt and enjoying the way the tension in his muscles gradually dissipated. As he was finishing his drink the gala guests started to arrive. It was time to charm donors and let rich old ladies flirt with him. Joy. Oh joy.

He'd done it all before, and it was easy to lose himself in the repetitiveness of it, but all the small talk and feigning interest in ski trips did little to quiet his mind. Every time he caught a glimpse of Darla, the desire to talk to her would grow. And, damn it, he didn't *want* to be sensible any longer.

Just start again. Such simple advice for dealing with self-inflicted deprivation. Could it be that easy? He wished it could. Especially when she looked so agonizingly right as she laughed at jokes he hadn't told and smiled at people who weren't him.

He politely excused himself from the trio of lawyers who'd been boring him out of his skull, then wove his way through the crowd of two hundred odd guests until he finally reached her side. Perhaps sensing him, she turned to meet his eyes.

He leaned down to bring his lips closer to her ear. "Can I have this dance?"

She drew back, her full lips pursed in a frown. "Are we supposed to be dancing?"

"Other people are."

"And I don't think those other people are dancing with their mentors."

The unexpected rejection started a sinking sensation in his stomach. "I thought it'd be a better way to pass the time. Never mind."

She caught his arm before he could leave and gave him

a tentative smile. "Come on."

He led her onto the dance floor and took her hand, his other hand resting on her hip. With how unsure of herself she was, he half-expected her to be stiff in his arms and awkward on her heels. Instead she moved with him fluidly, following his lead as if she could anticipate his movements. The same easy collaboration had made surgery with her an elegant process. He wondered how much of it was innate talent on her part and how much of it was an indefinable compatibility between them.

"You were wrong. I'm having fun," Darla said.

"I was wrong about a couple things. Guess you're good at surprising me."

"Do these events bring in a lot of money for the hospital?"

"Sort of. Mostly, it's a way to keep the donors we already have happy and feeling appreciated. Sometimes it draws in new donors too."

She tilted her head slightly and considered him for a moment. "Are you happy?"

The question caught him off guard, throwing his rhythm. He recovered quickly, but it left him feeling unsettled. "About what?"

"Your life. Where you are. The choices you've made."

"Yeah, I am." He wondered if he was lying. He was happy, wasn't he? His job was on the right course, provided things went well with Darla, and he was helping people every day. That had to count for something. Yet everything else in his life came as a distant, lonely second to work. It made it difficult to have any real sense of satisfaction, though he hadn't realized how bad it was until Darla came along. "Why do you ask?"

"I was just thinking about what Dr. White said. Maybe I shouldn't be going into trauma."

The fact that he didn't stumble in the dance when his heart stopped was some kind of miracle. He swore vehemently in his head, even as he fought to keep his face pleasant and his tone light. "Am I that bad of a mentor that you're abandoning your dreams already?"

"No!" She tipped her head back a little as she laughed, making her thick black curls slide off her bare shoulders and tempt him with the creamy bronze of her skin. "I've just never considered anything else. My mom always wanted me to follow in her footsteps and then go that extra step beyond."

Unable to think of a response at first, he fell silent. What Singh expected him to do was obvious and it was what would benefit him the most. But was it right? The thought of twisting her life path for his own benefit just left a bad taste in his mouth. He couldn't do it.

"Making life-altering decisions for somebody else's happiness isn't very smart," he said. "You need to decide what's going to make you happy. Otherwise you'll just fuck yourself over."

"Speaking from experience?"

"Eh. I've made my own share of mistakes, but luckily I've kept to my own path."

"And you don't regret that path?"

"No." The answer came automatically and, somewhat surprised, he knew it was the truth this time. Even if he wasn't satisfied, he couldn't regret it. Work wasn't really the problem. "I don't at all. I'm doing what I love, working towards other things I'll love even more."

"Like someday being Chief of Trauma Medicine?"

"That's the plan."

"You wouldn't be doing nearly as much surgery then."

"No, but I'd be helping a lot more people. There are all kinds of policies I could change. Like the twenty-eight hour shifts we put second-year residents through? That's terrible. We're better off being short-staffed than having staff who are going to make mistakes."

"But since everybody else had to go through that same agony, they're not going to want to see the newest crop of interns getting off easier."

"I know, and it's stupid. Just because we suffered doesn't mean the people who follow after us need to suffer too."

Darla leaned in closer against him, her breasts nudging his chest as she smiled up at him. "Look at you challenging the status quo. I never would have expected that."

"There's probably a lot about me you wouldn't expect."

"Like what?"

He hesitated. Work, sleep, followed by more work. It had been enough for years, dulling loss with monotony and ambition, but it sounded too empty. "I don't know. Stuff."

"Oh, that's good. That's really specific." She laughed again, giving his hand a squeeze in hers. "Come on. There's gotta be something."

"I'm a really good dancer?"

"I guess you are. Better than me, at least."

His hand at her hip drew her closer to him. Through his tux and her gown, he could feel the burn of her body, and his own ached for her. The rest of the gala might as well have melted away for all he cared.

He ducked, his lips an inch from her ear. "I think you're very good."

Chapter Ten

"After the clown incident, the children's hospital has been very reluctant about letting performers in." Nancy White looked thoughtful for a moment, then gave Darla a smile. "But I think it could be good. I'll talk to someone about it."

Elation filled Darla from head to toe, even taking her mind off her aching feet. The evening was nearly over and volunteers were starting to filter home. It had been her first chance to really talk with Dr. White, an opportunity she now relished. "That'll be great."

"What'll be great?" Jackson stopped a few feet away from them, his jacket slung over one arm, and his other hand in the pocket of his slacks. He looked as delicious as the gala's chocolate fountain and twice as bad for her.

"Darla suggested we bring in a cosplay group for kids."

Jackson glanced between the two of them with a faintly puzzled expression. "What's cosplay?"

"I'll let you explain. I have too much I need to handle here." White smiled at them both before making her exit.

"Cosplay is where people dress up like characters from superhero movies and comic books and stuff. It's really gotten big in the last couple years." Darla quirked a brow. "Exactly how old are you?"

"You're making me feel about a million years old right now, because I never heard that word before." He gave her a wry look. "You ready to go?"

She nodded and made her good-byes then strode beside him through the foyer.

The warmth of the afternoon had given way to a cool mountain night when they stepped outside. Without prompting, Jackson settled his jacket over her shoulders against the cold. She breathed in the desert air, which smelled and felt so different from back home in Chicago. Car exhaust and smog and all the city smells should have made them more similar, but each had a sense all its own.

The honor of geeks everywhere demanded she not let him distract her, though. "Maybe you haven't heard about cosplay yet, but superheroes have gone mainstream. I mean, everybody's seen the Marvel movies."

"I haven't."

"What?" She stopped in her tracks and gave him an incredulous look. "None of them?"

"Nothing recent. I stopped watching movies the first year of my residency."

"You mean in theaters?"

"No. At all." He rubbed the back of his neck. "I, uh, stopped getting into them like I used to."

She knew she was staring, but there was no helping it.

The first year of his residency would have been over five years before. No DVDs, no streaming video, nothing since then? Why would anyone choose that miserable boredom? Was this what his talk the other day had been about? "Are you kidding me? You need to spend your next day off catching up on pop culture."

"I wouldn't even know where to start."

"Then what are you doing for the rest of the night?"

At the car, Jackson opened the door for her, which made her smile. Of all the things people could say about Dr. De-Matteo at the hospital, somehow no one had ever caught onto his streak of chivalry. "Something tells me I'm watching movies."

Jackson took in the living room. The apartment was modestly-sized and all of the furniture looked like it had come from secondhand stores, but it was clean. About on par with what he expected of a couple first-year residents, who'd be old enough and busy enough to not have beer and pizza boxes everywhere. Going home with an intern to watch comic book movies had to be one of the stranger things he'd ever done, but he found it increasingly difficult to say no to Darla.

"So did you have fun?" he asked her.

"Yeah, but I'm regretting these heels now." She sat down on the couch and shifted her floor-length skirt around so she could pull off a shoe. When Jackson took a seat she held her foot up to wriggle her big toe, which had managed to work itself through her hose during the night. "Ugh."

He grinned. "That's impressive. You danced right through your pantyhose."

"They're not pantyhose. Can you imagine trying to wrestle with pantyhose under a dress like this?" Realization of what she'd said washed over her face, and she closed her mouth, teeth snapping together with an audible click. "Can we forget I said that?"

"I'm sorry, but I don't think I'm going to be able to." The mental image of working his hands up under that dress to ease her out of her stockings was going to haunt him for the rest of the night, if not longer. He cleared his throat. "Anyway, I'm glad you had fun. I really hadn't thought you would."

"Why?"

"You seem…anxious around people."

"I am. A little. This wasn't about me, though. It was about the hospital."

"And was figuring that out what made your bedside manner so much better?"

She looked down at her hands in her lap, a warm smile softening her face. "A little. I helped my neighbors' kid when she was having an allergic reaction, and all that fear and worry just disappeared. I had a job to do and being calm was the best way to do it."

"It helps. You're pretty compassionate, though. I don't think you should try to smother that human touch entirely."

"I'm not." Her heels now cast off, she left the couch to rifle through a shelf of DVDs next to the TV. "Now what do you like? Gritty and dark? Sci-fi action movies? World War Two? Shakespeare?"

Had this been some kind of trick? "I thought we were

watching something with superheroes."

"We are, but they're all different. So what are you into?"

He tipped his head to the side to look at the covers, trying to gauge something about them from the artwork, but it wasn't very helpful. "I guess I'm partial to Shakespearean tragedies."

She put the rest of the DVDs back. "Ooh, beneath that cold exterior beats the heart of a poet. I like it."

He frowned at her description, wondering if it was worth it to argue with her. "What are we watching?"

"Thor."

Rather than ask what the hell Norse gods had to do with Shakespeare, he bit his tongue. Part of him worried that trading valuable sleep time to watch a movie would make it impossible to actually enjoy it, but that worry was soon forgotten as he found himself engrossed in the story. By the end, he had to admit she was right about them having appeal for everyone.

Darla turned off the TV and dropped the remote before turning to face him on the couch. "You liked it, didn't you?"

"I liked it." The earnest concern in her eyes gave him the sudden urge to kiss away her worries. He leaned back from her, distancing himself from temptation. "Of course, we just watched it so you could drool over Thor, right?"

She scoffed with such offense he had to laugh. "Are you kidding? He's a great hero, but Thor isn't who I drool over in this movie."

"Oh, I see how it is now. Loki? I should've known. Women always want the bad boy." He paused to try to hide his amusement, doing his best to look serious. "But I think lusting after a genocidal maniac might be pushing it."

This time it was her turn to laugh, and she gave him a playful nudge with her elbow. "It's not like that. It's more like the lady version of wanting to rescue the damsel in distress."

"The villain isn't a damsel in distress."

"But movies don't make heroes emotionally vulnerable in the same way, and that's what appeals about the bad guy. It's not him being evil, it's his pain. He's hurt and looking for something. If he just let himself be loved, he could be saved."

Jackson glanced at the screen. Had they watched the same movie? "Saved from what?"

"Himself."

There was something in the way she said the word. This time he couldn't resist touching her. His hand cupped her cheek, his thumb stroking her skin. "Are we still talking about the movie?"

"Well, everybody could use a little saving now and then." Her eyes closed as she leaned into his touch, and he had the urge to kiss her eyelids and feel the brush of her lashes.

"What do I need saving from?"

His fingers slid from her cheek to the side of her neck, lightly tracing the lines of her body to memorize them through touch. She melted back against the couch and rolled her head, exposing more of her neck to his touch.

She was quiet for so long that he began to wonder if she'd respond at all before her eyes opened a slit. "Being a stick in the mud who only ever wants to do things the same way?"

His fingertips just barely teased behind her ear and at the fine hairs of her nape. It was the lightest touch he could manage without breaking contact, but it still flooded his body with heat. "Is that what you think of me?"

"I'm not sure, but it seems like you try really hard to make people think that."

He drew his hand away, torn between what he needed to do and what he wanted. "Maybe. I might be compensating a little."

She licked her lips, her heavy-lidded eyes never wavering from his. "Compensating for what?"

"For occasionally being very, very unprofessional."

Jackon's hand came back, this time burying itself in her hair. Her eyes widened a millisecond before his lips were on hers, and she shut them to focus purely on the kiss. It started out soft and almost hesitant, their lips brushing and caressing each other, before Jackson seemed to make up his mind. His mouth crushed hers in demand, and she moaned as her lips parted, opening herself up to him and the sweetness of his need. The tight control he kept on himself and everything around him was slipping, and she reveled in being swept up in the storm. The pounding of her heart in her ears grew louder, becoming a vibration through her whole body, until she had to break the kiss to gasp for breath.

Her head still spinning, she drew her cheek against his and let her breath tickle at his ear. "Is this unprofessional?" Her teeth caught his earlobe, worrying it before she sucked it between her lips.

They were close enough she could feel the rumble of his groan in his chest. "Pretty sure it is."

"Good. I think I like you unprofessional."

She found his lips with hers, giving herself up to the moment. The touch of his tongue against hers made her shudder, and she tangled with it, not so much to take over the kiss as to just keep feeling the struggle for dominance. His fingers ran through her hair, playing with the locks and making her toes curl. Instinctively, she pressed closer to him, trying to bridge every bit of distance still between them. One of his hands rested on her knee, sending electric shocks of arousal up her thigh to her core.

This time he broke the kiss, but he didn't pull away far, moving to her throat. "We shouldn't do this."

"If you don't think we should, then you can stop."

His lips followed her pulse back up to her ear to tease it. "I don't want to."

She laid her hand on his knee and squeezed, in part to stop her fingers from inching up any higher. "Then we might have a problem."

Each time his lips brushed her skin, she felt another bit of rationality slip away. Her thoughts were tumbling into one another until they didn't even form words, just impulses. Need. Desire. Something more tender and so new and dangerous she didn't want to acknowledge it was there at all.

He dragged her long skirt up until his hand could slide under it. The first brush of his fingers above the line of her stocking made the muscles in her thighs tremble from the unbearable anticipation. Had she ever felt so aware of the throb of blood through her veins, or the way the heat of it settled between her thighs? She doubted it. Certainly, she'd never been so tempted to ignore hospital policies.

Her hand caught his before it could travel any higher and nudged it back. "Whoa. Okay. Yeah, we should stop."

He drew away immediately, dragging his hand through his thick brown hair, which had taken on a fairly wild appearance since they started kissing. His olive-toned skin was flushed, his pale green eyes dilated. God, the man was sex personified. "Probably. Sorry if I crossed a line."

"You didn't. I was about to."

He went still, like a big cat spotting prey. The hungry look he gave her made her mouth go dry. "Were you? What were you going to do?"

She thought longingly of the chilled champagne flutes she hadn't touched at the gala and how badly she needed something to cool off despite the air conditioning in her apartment. "I don't think I can talk about them out loud," she teased.

He shrugged a little, one corner of his mouth curving up in a smile. "You don't have to, but I hate not knowing things."

Oh, the things she wanted to know about him. The temptation of his lips was far too much, and she needed to lean in to taste them one more time. With the way his arms automatically moved around her, he had to be suffering in the same way.

No matter how much she told herself this was a bad idea, she couldn't break the kiss. She felt helplessly dragged along by her body's reactions, like her craving for him was some compulsion that overtook everything else. This time there was no holding back. She slid her fingers up his thigh until they found the growing bulge through his slacks, and his groan sent an answering shudder through her. The heat of his arousal through the cloth was mesmerizing, and she traced the shape of his shaft with her fingertips again and again until she thought she could have sculpted him.

His hand cupped her breast, cradling the weight of the mound in his palm as his thumb sought out her satin-covered nipple. That touch sent tingles across her skin, flooding her veins with heat that left her body yearning. He grasped her waist with his other hand and tugged her closer, and she moved willingly to climb into his lap. She tugged her narrow skirt up to her knees so she could straddle him, her last shreds of self-control now lost.

He skimmed his hand from her waist around to the small of her back, then lower to grip her ass. The touch made her gasp into the kiss, and her hips rolled. She was rewarded by another quiet groan from him. Wicked possibilities began racing through her head, of riding him on the couch or taking him in her mouth.

There was the familiar sound of feet heavily tramping up the stairs outside. Before she had a chance to fully process it, Jackson had lifted her out of his lap and set her away from him. Legs tangled up with her skirt, she tried to sort herself out so she could sit properly again.

When she looked semi-decent, she narrowed her eyes at him. "What's wrong?"

"Your roommate could see us."

No one was opening the door, and she was fairly sure Brandon wouldn't be home for hours yet. Telling Jackson that was beside the point, though. They had to work together and men like him didn't fall for women like her anyway. She had felt so confident all night long, it had been easy to forget that she wasn't Cinderella at the ball. Reality came crashing down, crushing all those stupid little fantasies and hopes she'd let herself build up.

She tipped her head back over the couch to look toward the door, which remained as shut as ever. "My roommate isn't the only other person who lives in this building."

"Yeah, I know. That was stupid of me." He rubbed his hands over his face. "I really should go home."

"Okay." Still stinging, she stood up and avoided looking at him. She couldn't blame him for being concerned about being seen together like this, but that didn't make his extreme reaction hurt any less. Finding something else to talk about could, at the very least, distract from the rejection. She sought something to say, latching onto the first thing to come to mind. "They don't give us first years much of a break between shifts anyway. I hope I can get some sleep."

"You probably won't. Remember what you said about insomnia?"

She made a sound of disgust, hoping he was wrong. "God, how does anyone survive this?"

"When you get those little gaps between patients, knock back some coffee as fast as you can and then go to sleep in an on-call room." There was gentle concern in his voice, which soothed her bruised ego. "The caffeine will take about half an hour to kick in, and so you'll wake up better energized than you would from a regular nap."

She smiled weakly, wishing it was that easy. If she tried it, she'd be a jittery mess by the time she woke up and would quite likely have a complete anxiety attack a few hours later. Doctors who could tolerate caffeine didn't know how good they had it. "Where'd you learn that trick?"

"I can't remember who told me now, but there've been a couple studies on it."

Considering all the trouble he'd given her for vague

citations, she had to laugh. A little bit of hurt and worry wrapped around her heart let go with it, the worst of the awkwardness of the moment gone. "Now you're starting to sound like me. How can you be sure if it's only been a couple?"

He smiled at her teasing. "Because I've carried out hundreds of experiments with it on myself over the years."

"Hundreds? Everybody told me it got easier after you were an attending."

"It is. I just push myself a little harder than everybody else."

"Why?"

"How else could I be the best?"

That couldn't possibly be all there was to it. She'd been around too many doctors in her life and seen how competitive they could be. Nearly all of them wanted to be the best. Most of them still had lives. None of them, as near as she'd seen, pushed themselves with the same fervor as Jackson did.

What was he trying to make up for?

Chapter Eleven

The tapping of Dr. Elizabeth McGaffey's cane announced her presence in the hall before Jackson actually saw her. She was in her late sixties and despite multiple knee surgeries and the fact that she'd never run for an operating room again in her life, she remained one of the best trauma surgeons he had ever known.

She drew up alongside him, then gestured for him to walk with her. Jackson grabbed his morning coffee.

"How are things working out with Morales?"

Memories of Darla in his lap and the taste of her lips under his instantly overcame any other thought. Damn, it was pathetic how badly he wanted her. Dangerous, too. The only thing that came near to eclipsing his interest was the rising tide of guilt he was sure would drown him. "Fine." His voice was tight as he struggled to maintain a properly professional tone. "She's going to be a good surgeon."

McGaffey raised one sparse white eyebrow with a wry

little smile. "You don't sound like it's fine."

"There's a little personal conflict with her. It's nothing big."

"The two of you don't get along?"

Relief washed over him like a cool rain on a hot night. Her assumption wasn't entirely off the mark, considering some of the bickering between them, but a thousand arguments couldn't compare to the threat of one kiss from Darla. "Yeah, that's it. We're not compatible at all."

"Really? I thought the two of you had a lot in common. That was part of why I recommended she seek you out."

He nearly choked on his sip of coffee. "What do you think we have in common?"

"You're very driven, have long-term goals, occasionally lack some necessary introspection…"

He frowned at that. "What? Are you serious?"

McGaffey clucked her tongue, grinning. "If you were more introspective, you'd have figured it out already. You focus more on other people and fixing things for them than you do on yourself."

"I'm a surgeon. Getting my ego out of it is part of what makes me so good at it."

"What an incredibly humble thing to say," she deadpanned. "You're one of the most egotistical men I've ever met—"

He held up a hand to object, but she cut him off. "Easy there, Jackson. I wouldn't have you any other way."

He had to laugh at that, then gave McGaffey a warm look. The older woman's acerbic moods and sarcastic sense of humor had made her infamous during his own residency, but he loved her the way she was, like the snarky grandmother he'd never had. It was a relief to see the years hadn't mellowed her. "How can I be egotistical and fixated on other people?"

"Because you think you're the only one who can solve their problems. And then you don't have to worry about your own problems."

Some of his good humor cooled. "I don't have any problems."

McGaffey only looked amused by his denial. "Of course not. You're just perfect."

He drained the rest of his coffee in a long swallow, winced at the burn of it, and tossed the disposable cup in a trash can as they walked past it. "That's not what I said. I've never said that. Why the hell does everybody think that?"

"Because actions speak louder than words, and you don't let yourself be flawed."

"I've messed up plenty of times."

She stopped walking and leaned heavily on her cane, her face wrinkled with concern. "A few mistakes over a lifetime, but you dwell on them like capital crimes."

"What hell else should I do? Pretend it never happened?"

Instead of answering right away, McGaffey just drilled him with the kind of stare most interns did their damned-est to avoid. The silence stretched uncomfortably until she spoke again. "You mean Amy."

Just her name still had the power to knock the wind out of him, and he wished she could have stayed silent. There was no denying it, though, and he nodded. "Nobody will let me forget it and...and I shouldn't. All that's left of her is a memory."

"It's not your fault, Jackson." She was using her bedside

manner voice now. Soft, reassuring, and he hated it.

"How do you know? We don't know how things would have happened if I never got involved with her."

"I know because I've seen a lot of people die over the years. A lot of things can kill a person, but being loved was never one of them."

"Maybe they were being loved by the right people."

"You're one of the right people."

He scoffed. "Funny how that didn't keep her safe."

"I'm not saying you can save everyone, but you can offer them love and support. You probably—"

"Can we stop talking about me?" He hated to interrupt her, but wherever that sentence was going he couldn't handle hearing it. "Let's get back to Morales."

McGaffey paused, thin lips pursed in a frown, then she nodded. "Well, a lot of what I said applies to her too. You have things in common, remember?"

It took him a moment to pick up the thread. What had they been talking about before McGaffey mentioned Amy? Ah, yes. His ego. "Oh for God's sake. She's the last person in the world to think she's perfect."

A startled look passed over McGaffey's face, her eyes focused over his shoulder. "What makes you say that?"

He hesitated. It would have been smarter to not say anything at all. He couldn't explain how he'd been thinking about Darla far too much and trying to puzzle her apart like an especially challenging surgical approach. Talking about seeking out extra patients just to help boost Darla's confidence or watching her come to life like a sunrise when she succeeded at something sounded too revealing of his own feelings. Describing how she finally seemed to recognize her own beauty the night before would definitely be too much. He didn't dare try to explain that he thought her ego was too small mainly because he thought she was amazing. He grasped for something else to say instead. "She's insecure. It's probably her biggest weakness."

McGaffey finally looked him in the eyes again, though it wasn't him she was speaking to. "Hello Morales."

His stomach dropped into his feet and he spun to face Darla. God, he was an idiot. Of all the explanations he could have given, he picked one that sounded horrible to overhear.

Judging by the tense way Darla held herself, her face an almost expressionless mask, she must have heard at least his last comment. How she could think there was anything wrong with herself, he didn't know. Her scrubs couldn't hide the full perfection of her curves, particularly not after he'd seen them flaunted in that dress. She had her glasses on again and her lips looked just as tempting without the red lipstick. Her hair was back in its signature ponytail, but still looked soft and inviting, too. The sensory memory of how it had felt sliding between his fingers made him clench his hands.

"Hi Dr. McGaffey, DeMatteo."

He cleared his throat. "Morales. Did you get enough sleep last night?"

She didn't move in his direction. "I'm fine."

So many doubts and worries had plagued him since they'd kissed, he'd been sure he'd run out of worst case scenarios to obsess over. Darla being hurt and hating him was a new one, and he felt just a little ill wondering just how badly he'd fucked up. "I guess we'd better get our rounds going. Talk to you later, McGaffey."

A little further down the hall, he took her patient updates

from her. There didn't look to be anything surprising or worrying in any of them, to his relief. At least he could focus on a single disaster at a time.

"Good." He handed the tablet back to her. "Have you tried that trick with the coffee and the nap yet?"

Her skin actually went paler, and he could see her jaw clench. "No."

So much for trying for a neutral conversation. He forged ahead anyway, needing something to fill the strained silence. "It helps. I doubt I would've made it through my residency without it."

"That's nice."

"Listen, about last night…"

"It was a mistake. It won't happen again. Don't talk about it. I know."

Her flat, cold tone stung as badly as her words, and for a moment, he could only gape at her. "That isn't what I was going to say."

"No? Were you going to say it nicer to my face?"

"I wasn't going to say anything like that at all, to your face or otherwise."

"Then what?"

He froze, searching his mind. Was he going to say something like that? There were a few different versions of what he was going to say that he'd practiced, and now he couldn't remember any of them. "I'm a little worried about doing anything that could detract from your education."

Her eyes narrowed behind her glasses. "Yeah, that's the nice version. I won't bring it up if you don't, okay?"

"Darla."

"What?"

He was silent. More than anything else, he wanted to take her into his arms and kiss her again and reassure her that whatever she'd overheard, it wasn't meant to be hurtful. Just his own blundering attempt to cover up how he really felt. It should have been obvious to her, but it wasn't. And he'd made it all so much worse.

"Nothing. Let's just work."

Chapter Twelve

S hopping still didn't fill her with whatever thrill she was supposed to get out of it, but Darla had to admit that looking at clothes with Rachel and Nikki did improve her mood.

"I just don't know what the hell to think. He was talking about how *insecure* I am behind my back, when the last time he saw me I was actually feeling pretty good about myself. And then he acts like he's doing me a favor, saying he doesn't want to distract from my education by pretending nothing happened between us." Darla held up a tiny negligee that she was uncertain she could get over her head, let alone the rest of her. "But he couldn't get enough of me at my apartment." Well, right up until he thought her roommate was approaching. Then he shut down quicker than a quarantine after a call from the CDC.

Nikki pulled the negligee out of her hands and replaced it with a pair of green and white striped boy shorts. "Reminds me of dating girls in the closet. They're so hot and cold all the time, always afraid of getting caught, and that just makes them all the more desperate when you're together."

Rachel shook her head, clicking her tongue in disapproval. "I'm so glad I've put those days of drama behind me."

"Preach." Nikki kissed Rachel on the cheek.

Darla sank down into one of the overstuffed chairs tucked around the lingerie store. She assumed they were for waiting boyfriends and husbands, but maybe sitting and brooding over their love lives was what all women did while underwear shopping. "So I should just forget about him then?"

"Oh, I never said that. Did I say that?" Nikki dropped a few more articles of clothing into Darla's lap, then continued her search. "Whether or not you want to deal with the drama is entirely up to you."

"I just hate feeling like a loser."

Rachel leaned down and fixed her with a hard look. "So stop acting like one. Pick out some clothes you like. Feel sexy and awesome. You don't need him to feel good about yourself."

Darla considered the clothing in her lap, then stretched a pair of black lace panties between her hands. "I spend sixteen hours a day in scrubs. Clothes can't make much of a difference for me."

"Hey, you're not the only woman in the world who's had a shitty uniform for work," Nikki called over from the display she'd wandered to. "That's why we're looking at panties and bras. You wear that under a potato sack, and you'll *still* feel like a sexy bitch."

Darla wasn't sure she felt *like a sexy bitch*, but two full shifts without working with Jackson had dulled the pain a little. Enough that when she had to do rounds with him, it was just a vague ache.

"Everything looks good, Mr. Peterson." Jackson smiled at their patient, the construction worker she'd cried in front of on her first day. "I don't see any reason not to discharge you today."

Mr. Peterson looked like he might be the one to cry now. He reached over to squeeze his wife's hand tightly. "I can't thank you enough. I really thought that fall had crippled me."

"Well, we can't take all the credit. Our neurology department certainly helped there, but Morales and I did do our best. Do you have any other questions or concerns?"

"When can I get back to work?"

"That's best decided by your physical therapist. Morales?"

She mentally ran through everything she'd done for the day, then bit her lip to stop from swearing in front of the patient. "I forgot to set up the referral."

Jackson drew his brows together. "Then why don't you go do that?"

She ran to set up the referral and enter the paperwork for releasing the patient. There was so much to do and it just kept piling up around her she wanted to scream. A glance at the clock on the wall verified her shift was nearly over. If she took a pill and started falling asleep, at least there wouldn't be any harm from it, assuming she made it home.

She supposed passing out on a bus and riding around in it all night could be a problem.

"Hey, Morales."

She looked up to see Richard Mevlyn looming over her, smiling like he had a secret. That knowing look in his eyes had her shrinking in on herself automatically, her mind running through all possible scenarios. Had she messed up somewhere with a patient? Did someone find out she was planning on switching programs at the end of the year?

"Hello, Dr. Mevlyn." Her mouth was bone dry.

His smile grew wider. "You and DeMatteo were getting pretty close at the gala."

Shit. Maybe Jackson hadn't been overly paranoid after all. "I don't know what you're talking about."

He shrugged. "I guess girls like you have to take what attention they can."

She stiffened, a cold rage flooding her veins. Punching an attending surgeon would probably be bad for her career, but the urge was overwhelming. She wanted to ask what "girls like her" meant, but there was no possible answer that she actually wanted to hear. She bit her tongue.

His smile wilted slightly, likely disappointed that she hadn't risen to the bait. "I thought it was a good idea to warn you about DeMatteo. He likes going after the vulnerable."

She narrowed her eyes. "He has no interest in me. I don't need your warnings."

"Oh." Mevlyn straightened up, looking thoughtful. "Well. Never mind then."

"Thank you for your concern." She said it as politely as she could, hoping that would be the end of it, but she could see by the expression on Mevlyn's face it wouldn't be.

"I did want to ask you a question." He smiled again.

Her skin was trying to crawl right off her body, and she wished fervently that he'd leave her alone soon. Other people at the hospital seemed to enjoy the smarmy attention of Mevlyn, but she couldn't see the appeal. "What's that?"

"I couldn't place your accent. Where are you from?"

Her *accent*? She was taken aback for a moment. "Uh, Chicago."

"No, I mean originally."

Under the best of circumstances, she would have found his approach frustrating. Sometimes it could just be friendly ignorance, but the way Mevlyn looked at her gave her a gross feeling. It wasn't helped by the fact that Jackson had warned her about him.

"I've got a lot of work. Excuse me." She grabbed the phone again to pretend to make another call. Anything to avoid having to speak to him a moment longer. That seemed to do it and he finally walked away. She glared at his back, then noticed Jackson coming toward her. Before he got there a petite brunette caught up to him and grabbed him into a hug.

Jackson looked pleasantly surprised by this, and the woman smiled up at him. "You're coming out with me tonight!"

Three days and he already had a new woman. Darla had no right to be jealous, but she could still feel it prickling away at her. The least he could do is not flaunt it right in her face.

Jackson sighed. "Eliza, I'd love to, but I've just had a really busy day. I'd rather go home and go to sleep."

"And that's why you're coming with Chris and me. You're going to turn into an old man before your time at this rate."

Chris? Well, maybe it wasn't someone he was hooking up with, if they were going out with another person. She thought she could vaguely remember him talking about his friend Chris before. The woman could be Chris's girlfriend, then. Silly as it was, she hoped that was the case.

"Morales, do you have Mr. Peterson's referral?"

The question startled her out of her thoughts. "Yes, Dr. DeMatteo. And he's all set to be discharged."

Eliza looked at her in interest, her expression warm and inviting. "Oh, is this your mentee?"

Jackson nodded, looking reluctant. "If you want to call her that."

"I'm Jackson's sister, Eliza. It's nice to finally meet you. Darla, right?"

"Um, yeah. Hi." Had Jackson been talking about her? That introduction eased some of the tension in her shoulders. His sister. Not a girlfriend. He'd been talking about her to his sister. Then she felt a flash of annoyance at herself. She had no reason to be relieved.

"You should come out with us, too. I imagine the hospital's working you to death. I remember Jackson's horror stories from his residency."

The invitation took a few seconds to sink in. When it did, her eyes widened in horror. Having to deal with him at work all day had been bad enough, but actually socializing with him was too much. "No way. It's not...I mean, I don't mind...I..."

Jackson looked thoughtful. "You should come with us, Morales."

She closed her mouth rather than try to stammer through more protests. And what about all his bullshit about keeping their distance? "Can I talk to you privately for a second?"

He excused himself from his sister and walked a few feet away with Darla. His expression was bland. She couldn't tell what he was thinking and that only annoyed her more.

"What the hell are you doing?" She kept her voice to a hiss as an added precaution against being overheard. "I thought you didn't want to detract from my education."

He spread his hands in a gesture of futility. "No, I said I was a little worried about it. It's a friendly night out. Can't we have that?"

"The gala was a friendly night out, too." And that had ended so very *friendly* she had to force herself not to dwell on the memories. "Do you even want me to go or are you just playing weird games with me?"

His hands dropped to his sides, his posture growing defensive. "I'm not playing games. You seemed really upset before, and I thought this might be fun for you."

"So it's a pity invite." She crossed her arms. "You want me to go to make you feel better about making me feel bad."

"No." He gave his head a small shake, and she thought she detected a slight roll to his eyes. "I wanted a chance to make things better than how we'd left them. You don't have to go if you don't want to."

She hesitated. The thought of taking the bus home and eating ramen noodles before passing out and coming back for another sixteen hour shift wasn't remotely appealing. She raised her chin, doing her best to look down her nose at him despite their height difference. "Oh, I'm going. Just don't think it absolves you of anything."

This time he definitely rolled his eyes. "I wouldn't dream of it."

Chapter Thirteen

"Cascata's a gorgeous place for a golf course, but you can't even see it from the road driving in. Just another rich boy's playground hidden from the rest of us." Chris wrapped an arm around Eliza's shoulders, leaning back in the booth. "Wasting water aside, I prefer the desert as it's meant to be."

After leaving the hospital, Chris had suggested they stop at a bar and grill in a Strip casino for burgers before continuing onward. Jackson had offered to buy Darla a beer, but she'd stuck with her water and used it to wash down a pill. Was it medication or did she just have a headache? It was hard to quell the medical curiosity, but there was no polite way to ask.

"The mountains are beautiful." Darla swirled a French fry in her ranch dressing before popping it in her mouth. "I just don't really know what you'd do in the desert for fun, though. Are there a lot of walking trails out there?"

Eliza smiled and nodded. "Tons. If you like hiking, there're a lot of options."

"Hiking's okay. I jog around the park near my apartment when I can, but some of the mountains here look pretty intense."

"You can take riding trails too." Chris's eyes were lit like an evangelist about to save a soul.

To Jackson's amusement, Darla wrinkled her nose. "Me and horses don't mix so well."

He leaned over a little closer to her, lowering his voice as if sharing a special secret. "Me neither. Watch out for these two, though. They don't like to take no for an answer."

That close to her he could smell the clean scent of her skin and the faint traces of perfume. A little like vanilla, which had him wishing he could taste her skin as well. She shivered at his nearness, but didn't draw away. As impossible as anything between them still was, he couldn't help being relieved she still felt the connection. If nothing else, he couldn't leave her thinking he didn't find her absolutely beautiful.

Chris wadded a straw wrapper into a ball and threw it at his head. It bounced off his cheekbone, making him squint. "How many times have I forced you on a horse?"

"I think the first time was once too many."

Eliza ignored them, speaking to Darla. "Did you notice the gun range across the highway when you went to Cascata?" At Darla's shake of her head, Eliza beamed with delight. "Well, they've really expanded it since I lived here before. Now there's a clubhouse where you can get dinner and blow things up."

Darla cocked a skeptical brow and shot Jackson a look.

He shrugged, not knowing anything about it. "Is that a joke?"

"No, it's absolutely true." Chris accepted the bill from the server and pulled out his wallet. "They actually advertise it as 'blow shit up' on their website."

Jackson offered a few bills to Chris. "Will that cover Darla and me?"

"Yeah, that looks about right."

"I can pay for my own food," Darla protested.

Jackson shook his head, remembering the low pay of his years as a resident far too well. She could probably afford a burger and fries, but why couldn't she just let him take care of it? "Don't worry about it. It's too much of a pain in the ass to have everybody fighting over the bill."

She looked a little uncertain, as if she didn't trust the gesture. "Thank you. Anyway. That shooting range sounds like something out of a bad comedy."

Jackson chuckled at her skepticism. "I've never heard of that one, but there's a place just over the state border in Arizona that's a greasy spoon slash shooting range. Some kid accidentally shot one of the instructors, and he was flown to UMC for care."

Eliza nudged Chris to slide out of their side of the booth. "Yeah, so you can fire an AR-15 while ordering a milkshake, but you can't smoke while you're drinking it."

Darla shot Jackson an exasperated look. "I'm never going to understand Las Vegas."

Chris led the way out of the restaurant and back into the casino proper. "What's there to understand? It's the most normal place on Earth."

Darla's carefree laugh in response reminded him of how

she'd laughed after the gala, before reality intruded again. "You've never lived outside of Nevada, have you?"

Eliza leaned in against Chris's side and gave his arm a squeeze. "Someday we'll build the cabin of our dreams in Yosemite."

"What, you mean inside the park?"

Jackson had to grin and moved a little closer to Darla, slowing his gate to match hers. "They've got dreams of setting up a ranch. It'll probably involve moving, but it won't be to Yosemite."

Chris scoffed. "Says you. If you're gonna dream, dream big."

Darla stared at Chris a moment, then turned her disbelieving eyes on Jackson. "They are joking, right?"

He shrugged. "Eliza is. I couldn't tell you what Chris is actually thinking."

Outside rush hour traffic was over, the constant flow of vehicles on the Strip picking up speed. Horns blared here and there while people wove between lanes as if playing a particularly dangerous game of Candy Crush. Tourists crowded the sidewalks, many of them with large drinks in their hands thanks to the city's liberal open container laws. It was a combination that never failed to put Jackson on edge.

Chris stopped. "What do you think about doing the Big Shot?"

Jackson followed his eyes to the Stratosphere Tower that loomed over the city like the world's tallest toothpick. "I dunno. You have to wait so long, and the ride only takes about thirty seconds."

Eliza put her hands on her hips. "Absolutely not. You guys can do that if you want, but I've been talked into enough traumatizing rides."

"Is that the one on top of the Stratosphere that shoots you into the air and then you drop back down over a hundred feet?" Darla was looking at her phone rather than the tower.

Jackson nodded. "That's the one."

"And it's got a g-force of four when you're dropping and people with back problems and heart conditions shouldn't ride it?"

"Yeah, that's right."

She shuddered. "I'll stick with Eliza on the ground, thanks."

"Did you just google that?"

She put the phone back in her pocket and gave him a defiant look. "I like knowing things."

He laid a hand on her arm, feeling her shiver under his touch, and stepped closer to her. God, she was appealing. "I'm not complaining."

"Oh." The word came out as almost a sigh. Then she pulled herself free and coughed into her fist. "This has been great, but I really should go home. I have to catch sleep when I can."

"I'll take you," Jackson said automatically, then wanted to smack himself in the face. Of course, he had to take her. He'd driven her from the hospital and she had no other way to leave, short of a cab or waiting hours for the bus system to function.

"God, Jackson. Your boringness is rubbing off on her. That should be criminal," Chris teased.

"If I'm so boring, why do you guys keep hanging out with me?"

"Because we're hoping to cure you, obviously."

The screech of locked brakes and sliding tires cut through the air, followed by crunching metal. Before he had fully processed the sound, Jackson grabbed onto Darla and dragged her back from the edge of the sidewalk, his arms like vices around her as if just holding tight enough would keep danger at bay. It took him a moment to realize the accident hadn't been near them, and she wasn't at risk.

"Jackson?" Darla remained still in his arms, concern clear in her voice.

Rather than try to explain his reaction, he released her to head toward the upheaval, but even without his arms around her she stayed with him. Behind him, he could hear Eliza calling 911 on her phone.

Further down the road a truck had over-corrected at the corner and rolled into a light post. Glass littered the ground like raindrops. Mercifully, no other vehicle looked to have been involved.

The driver was crawling out of his side of the cab, looking dazed and bruised. A gash near his hairline was oozing blood down his face. When they got closer, Jackson saw that it was a double-cab truck, with the backseat crushed by the weight of the vehicle on top of it.

"I'm fine. I'm fine." The driver weaved a bit on his feet. It was difficult to tell how much of that was from injury and shock and how much was related to the stench of alcohol on his breath.

From inside the crushed backseat, a muffled little voice cried, "Help!"

"Here, I'll handle this," Chris said, jogging up to the driver. A veterinarian was probably better than nothing, at least.

Eliza started barking for people to stay back. Like Chris, Jackson's sister was good in a crisis.

Ignoring the driver for the moment, Jackson pulled off his jacket and crouched down to inspect the truck. Gas dripped everywhere—the tank must have been punctured during the roll—and wires from the busted light post were sparking. He covered his mouth with his hand, fighting back a few dozen other swear words. "Just stay calm. We need you to hold still in case you're hurt. Darla, I can't reach him to see how bad it is. Do you think you can?"

She crouched down beside him, shaking her head. "I'm not any smaller than you."

Did she honestly think that? He shot her an annoyed look as he sized up their physical differences. There was a hell of a lot of curve to her, but that was less likely to get in her way than broad shoulders. "You're a lot smaller than me. Will you do it?"

A torrent of emotions ran across her face all at once, her body frozen in the conflict.

The little voice from inside the crushed cab began to sob. "My leg's stuck."

Her jaw set, the fear and doubt vanishing. "Hold my purse." She stripped off the jacket she'd worn for the cool spring evening and then crawled through the front of the cab before working her way back to the boy.

Through the broken glass and crushed frame, there was too little room for him to see. He craned his neck, only able to catch glimpses of Darla's movements in the dark interior.

"There's gasoline all over everything in here. We need to get him out!" she called.

He cocked his head, straining to hear how close the

sirens were. "Moving him could aggravate a spinal injury. If he can't get out on his own, you'd better come out to wait for the ambulance."

"His spine won't do him a damn bit of good if he burns up!"

From inside, he heard several hard kicks until the driver seat was knocked forward and the little boy crawled out. He looked about seven, with blond hair sticking out in every direction on his head and pale blue eyes wide in shock. A bump on his forehead was starting to swell and darken with bruising. Even with no blood and all his limbs in working order, Jackson knew better than to trust appearances after a crash like that. Internal injuries could hide. He picked the boy up to protect him from the broken glass and looked over to his sister, who was off her phone and coming toward him.

"Eliza, take him and get back. There's a lot of spilled gas."

He passed the boy to her, then crouched to help Darla. As soon as she was free, Jackson pulled her into his arms, hugging her in part just to keep from yelling at her. In the same situation, could he have done any differently?

The driver sat on a patch of sidewalk free of fuel and glass, where Chris was doing his best to keep him still. "Could you get my wallet, too?"

Rage and adrenaline narrowed his vision down to a pinpoint. He released Darla from his arms, grabbed the driver by the front of his shirt, and dragged him to his feet. "What were you doing driving drunk like that? You could've killed people. You could've killed your son."

The man shoved back at him. "His mom's working and I couldn't leave him alone at home. He had his games to keep him busy."

Jackson unclenched one hand from the drunk's shirt and drew it back. Soft hands took hold of his arm to stop the punch. Darla gave a gentle pull. He blinked and looked around, noticing the crowd that had gathered around them as well as the welcome lights of a police cruiser in the distance.

He released the man and raised his voice. "Everybody get back. This could catch fire." He looked to the driver again, his lip curled with disgust. "Darla, you help Chris while we wait for the EMTs. I'll look at his son."

Once the ambulance arrived and he could leave them to their work, Eliza grabbed him into a fierce hug. He hugged her back, then sagged against the retaining wall beside the sidewalk.

Darla settled next to him. "Thank you for not getting arrested for assault. It's not worth it. He's a drunk driver who's going to pay for what he did."

"Yeah, right, he'll pay." Jackson scoffed. "He could've killed people, but their good luck means he'll probably just lose his license."

"You don't know that."

He shook his head wearily, the aftermath of another accident on a film loop running behind his eyes. No one died this time, but it didn't make the memories stop. "I've seen too many people get hit and even then there's no real justice. You can't undo the past."

"But losing his license might help prevent this from happening again. We can stop the past from repeating, right?"

He was quiet for a moment, then wrapped an arm around her shoulders. She curled in against his side like she'd been made to fit there. "I hope so."

Chapter Fourteen

Darla leaned against the cool glass of the window, watching the lights of the city pass by the car as she replayed the aftermath of the accident. There had been no complete panic on her part once the worst was done, and she wasn't sure if she could credit her medication or just getting better at handling stress. Maybe it didn't matter why, just so long as there was improvement.

Instead, it had been Jackson's reaction that had been the extreme one. When she turned from the window to look at him, he was drumming his fingers on the steering wheel with a restless look on his face. He wasn't trying to punch anyone, but he still seemed on edge and there'd been something more in the way he grabbed onto her than just safety.

"I feel kind of stupid asking this after everything that happened, but…" She trailed off. It seemed so manipulative, but it was probably for his own good, wasn't it? He'd just go home alone and bottle things up again otherwise.

His hands stilled. "What do you need?"

At least she didn't have to feign embarrassment when she answered him. "I was just thinking of maybe not going straight home. My roommate's at the hospital tonight, and I don't want to be alone."

He nodded a little and one of his fingers restarted its tapping. He didn't even seem to be aware of it. "Why don't you come back to my condo? It can take a while for the adrenaline rush to die down."

That wasn't what it was, she was sure. An adrenaline rush on beta-blockers wouldn't really work. She'd never been able to understand the thrill other people took in adrenaline rushes, since they just tended to leave her shaky and sweaty in the worst way, but this was different. Every nerve was on alert, her senses picking up tiny details she wouldn't have noticed before. Like the spicy masculine scent of him and the little bit of warmth coming off of his arm next to hers. If this was what excitement was like without the anxiety, she could see why it was addictive.

"That sounds good. Thanks."

Part of her still couldn't quite believe what she'd done. She'd crawled inside of a crushed truck and then kicked her way out again. *Her.* She never would have guessed she was capable of it until it had to be done. Rachel had told her that confidence came from being herself and feeling good about being herself. It turned out that being the kind of person who saved a child felt a thousand times better to her than being the kind of person who looked good in an evening gown.

"It's a lot more amped up like this than it is at the hospital, huh?" Darla asked.

His eyes left the road briefly to meet hers, the hungry look in them catching her like a fly in amber. *Something* was amped up, at least, but more than simple need reflected in his eyes. A hint of pain flashed in them before he refocused on the traffic. Whatever that hurt was, it made her ache to comfort him as badly as lust had her aching for other things.

"Yeah, it is." He shook his head, lips pressed tightly together. "I've had to stop for a few car accidents and it's always a little more…raw than it is coming in off an ambulance."

It sounded believable, but she was sure there was more to it. Something terrible had happened and yet he showed no sign of admitting it.

She took a deep breath and this time noticed something other than Jackson's scent. "There's less getting drenched in gasoline, anyway."

He sniffed at the air inside the car and made a face. "Shit. I forgot about that. You can take a shower at my place, and I'll throw your stuff in the wash."

Showering at his place? She'd be naked in an attending surgeon's home, which had to cross the boundaries he'd tried to put between them. She couldn't remember anything specific about showering under the anti-fraternization policy, but it surely broke the spirit if not the letter. Yet he'd suggested it. Just like he'd asked her to come out with him. Just like he kept looking at her like he wanted to eat her up. His comments about her she'd overheard before had to have been a misunderstanding. Pleasure bubbled up in her, considering that.

Caution tempered it, though. As good as it felt to be a bad influence on his self-control, those boundaries he'd tried to construct did serve a purpose in her favor. Getting transferred because of a relationship before she was ready to leave the hospital would complicate everything.

At his split-level condo he let her in and directed her downstairs to the bathroom. The condo was a rung or two up the socioeconomic ladder from her apartment, but still more modest than expected for a surgeon pulling in as many hours as he did. The few pictures scattered around the place looked to all be from childhood, and there were no signs of hobbies. She wondered what sins he thought he was paying for by depriving himself.

In the medicine cabinet, she found two bottles of women's body wash. One looked fairly fresh, and she guessed it had been left by Jackson's sister before she moved in with Chris. The other looked to be years old and had remained in the same spot for so long there was a faint dust ring around its base. Darla scrubbed the gasoline off in the shower with the newer body wash, taking no time to linger, then toweled herself dry. Only when she was wrapping the towel around herself did she realize the obvious problem. She looked down at the pile of clothes on the floor, poked it with her toe, and sighed.

She opened the door a crack to call out. "Uh? Jackson?"

His voice answered from the top of the stairs. "Yeah?"

"I'm not gonna have to wear a towel until my clothes are done, am I?"

"Shit, I forgot. One second."

A moment later he appeared at the door with a T-shirt. Jackson handed it to her through the cracked door and his eyes slid over her exposed skin, drinking her in as if he couldn't get his fill. His gaze worked its way thoroughly up to her eyes and her heart skipped a beat. "Your clothes?"

She licked her lips. "What?"

"I was going to put your clothes in the wash."

She winced. Of course. That was the only reason she was standing practically naked in front of him. "Right. Sorry."

She handed him her outer clothes, then shut the door. Being short worked in her favor for once. His shirt fell almost to her knees, and with her underwear it was as modest as most of the skirts she owned. She climbed the stairs again to find him in the kitchen, drinking a glass of wine.

When he saw her, he picked up a second glass and offered it. "Want some? Might help settle you after the excitement."

She shook her head. "I probably shouldn't. Alcohol doesn't mix well with medication I'm on."

He frowned at that and looked like he wanted to say something more before he took another sip off his wine. "You did good tonight. You kept your cool better than I did, at least."

She hopped up on the counter beside him and hooked her ankles together. "Got a thing against drunk drivers?"

"Lot of cases I see are the result of drunk driving. Did you know there were over eighty fatal car accidents in Las Vegas last year?" He finished off his wine and set the glass down again, avoiding her eyes. "Shitty parenting tends to set me off, too."

"Because of your parents?" There was more he wasn't saying, she just couldn't figure out what.

"Mine aren't really shitty, and my dad isn't a drunk. Just completely married to his work."

She gave him a nudge with one bare foot and smiled teasingly. "That doesn't sound familiar at all."

He caught her foot before she could pull it away. His

thumb rubbed back and forth along her arch, the sensation making her toes curl and her breath catch in her throat. "I don't have kids to neglect."

"No, just yourself."

"What makes you think that?" He trailed his fingers up from her foot, following the curve of her calf to behind her knee.

The tickle of his fingers sent a shock like lightning up her thigh and made her inhale sharply. "Just..." She trailed off and her eyes closed as he slid his hand under the shirt to massage the tense muscles of her thigh. "You don't seem to know how to have fun."

He chuckled and the warm, low sound was like velvet down her spine. "Haven't we had a lot of fun together already?"

"Not nearly enough."

Her eyes still shut, she felt him take her glasses off and set them aside. The first brush of his lips against hers was so brief she almost missed it. Hungry for more, she leaned forward into him, catching the back of his neck to pull him in. Without hesitation, his lips claimed hers and she opened to his onslaught. With the demanding explorations of lips and brief nibbles of teeth, she could feel the rest of the world falling away. The worries that plagued her at every turn were silenced, filling her mind with a dull roar of need instead. For the moment, there was just this. Just them.

His arms wrapped around her, holding her in place like steel bands. It could have so easily felt stifling, but with him it only made her feel safe. Her hands fisted the fabric of his shirt, tugging him closer in turn. He abandoned her lips, and she made a soft cry of protest that trailed into a sigh when he kissed down her throat. She tipped her head readily to invite him for more, the teasing brushes of his lips on her skin making her shiver. His teeth teased over her pulse point, which trembled with an unsteady beat.

He pressed one more kiss there, then took her lips again. This time she pressed forward into the kiss to fight him for control, feeling just as demanding as he was. Driven by instinct, she hooked her legs around him and was rewarded by the heat of his hard arousal when he rocked against her. Awareness of just how little separated their bodies made her whimper.

He broke the kiss with a gasp and nuzzled her cheek, not giving a spare inch of space between them. "Maybe I should stop neglecting myself." His voice was husky, almost a growl.

Without loosening his hold on her, he took one hand from the small of her back to cup her breast through the shirt. Her nipple hardened in anticipation a moment before his thumb swept over it to tease the little nub.

"Yes." The word came on an ecstatic sigh as she arched into his touch, unsure of what she was even saying yes to. Maybe to everything he could ever offer her.

Jackson took hold of the hem of the shirt and gave it a tug. She hesitated before squirming to get it out from under her and shrugged it off, hissing at the cold counter-top now against the bare skin of her thighs. Her body was tense with self-consciousness, her arms automatically moving in to cover some of her exposed skin. Clothing could flatter and hide so much, but now she felt dangerously on display, especially with him still fully dressed.

He frowned and stepped closer to her again. The tease of his lips and breath at her ear were warm enough to banish the chill of the counter. His hands slid down her arms, then caught her wrists to gently tug at them. "Please don't deprive me? There's nothing I'd rather see right now than you."

God, the man had no right to be so good at shutting her brain down. She nodded and relaxed her arms bit by bit, letting him pull them apart to expose her to his gaze. The last thing on her mind when she'd gotten dressed that morning was anyone looking at her in her underwear, but she was thankful for Rachel and Nikki's urges to be more fashionable. The black lace of her matching bra and panties set had seemed like a nice combination when she'd bought it. The raw desire in Jackson's green eyes as he gazed at her made her resolve to never wear boring underwear again, so long as there was a chance he might see her in it.

His fingers traced the lacy edge of her bra. "Is this what you wear under your scrubs?"

"It's what I was wearing under them today." And if it would get him to look at her like that, she'd fill her drawers with matching sets.

He groaned and shut his eyes, his face almost pained. "You have no idea how hard it's going to be to focus on work knowing that." He ducked and kissed the mound of one breast where it rose above the cup of her bra, then the other breast. "So beautiful." His light touches spread fresh warmth through her body, her throat tighter around each breath. Once he'd freed her from her bra, he teased at one nipple with his tongue before closing his lips around it. "So friggin' beautiful."

She tangled her fingers in his hair and moaned, rewrapping her legs and her other arm around him to hold him. "You actually make me feel like that."

"Good. I hope you never stop."

He abandoned her breasts to kiss lower down her body. The scrape of his stubble at her bare stomach sent unexpected flutters through her, and she tightened her legs around him. His hands caught her knees and pushed them further apart as he kissed lower, until his lips met the front lace of her panties. It was the thought of him there more than anything else that jolted her body with hunger and she bit her bottom lip.

He ran his fingers from her knee down the inside of her thigh and rubbed them against her wet folds through the lace. The lace was soft enough, but having it pressed against her like that by his fingers made every little ridge of it stand out against eager nerve endings. She braced her hands on the counter and slid forward, closer to the edge and him until she felt in danger of falling off. The firm grip of his free hand holding her settled that fear so all she had to concentrate on was Jackson.

The next pass of his fingers was firmer, pushing the lace ever so slightly between her outer lips. He kept teasing her until his middle finger pressed in to circle her clit. The scrape of the lace against such delicate skin was almost agonizingly good. She whimpered and rolled her hips, wordlessly begging him for more.

He caught the waist of her panties with his fingers and tugged, letting them slide down her legs until they caught on one ankle. The sheer audacity of what she was doing—in an attending surgeon's *kitchen*, for God's sake—hit her all at once. Her skin burning with a blush, she started to form the words to tell him they needed to move somewhere else, but she couldn't find her voice. Not when his lips were kissing up the inside of her thigh, inching closer and closer to where she ached for him.

At first he just kissed. His lips brushed her slick folds and gently stroked their way upward. Then he pressed more firmly and his tongue worked in to touch her for the first time. Slow, thorough explorations teased between the lips of her sex, then glanced over her clit.

She hissed at the direct touch at last and crept onto the very edge of the counter, watching him through heavy-lidded eyes. There was absolutely no way in hell there could be a future between them. It was risky because of work, impossible because she was going to leave the state, and irresistible all at once. She had to purposefully remind herself that it couldn't change anything, otherwise she was sure she'd lose her heart entirely. This felt too right with him. It was masochistic to even give in this much, but there was no way she could deprive herself entirely.

The tension climbed higher as he alternated between drawing circles around her clit with his tongue and stroking it directly. When his lips wrapped around the little nub to focus all his ministrations, she came crashing down with a startled cry. Her fingers twisted in his hair to hold him close, needing that touch to keep her anchored.

After the moment passed she leaned back on her elbows on the counter to try to catch her breath. Jackson straightened, pulling his shirt off in the same motion. Feeling shameless for the moment, she allowed herself to openly stare at him. The hard lines of his broad chest begged to be traced with fingers or her tongue. His arms were thick and well defined, the muscles cording up when he braced his hands on the edge of the counter and leaned forward over her.

She pushed herself up to meet him, sighing into the kiss. The taste and scent of her own orgasm on his lips was almost obscene in its intimacy. The hunger on his side was palpable, his body tense and ready.

"Do you want me, Darla?" he breathed against her cheek.

"Yes." It was a shockingly easy thing to say to him. Her hands slid down his body to open his belt, then she hesitated. Doubt and insecurity were difficult to shake. Even if it meant nothing, she had to be sure she was more than just a momentary convenience. She needed to be the object of his desire, not simply a tool to slake his need. "Do you want *me*?"

"How can you even doubt that?" He guided her hand to his arousal trapped by his jeans. An erection didn't really tell her what she wanted to know. "Do you want me inside you?"

At least that was an easy question. She whimpered, nodding, and turned to catch him in another kiss. She helped him work his jeans open and free him from his boxers before he rolled on a condom from his pocket.

He pressed into her slowly at first, stretching her around him, allowing her body time to adjust. The warm, thick feeling of his shaft inside of her comforted her in a way she'd never experienced with sex before. His next thrust was deeper, harder, and she moved to meet him, accepting everything he had to offer. It was almost too easy to find a rhythm with him, just as it had been on the dance floor at the gala. Or in the operating room. No fumbling, he didn't speed up when she wanted to go slower. Nothing but grace in motion.

The counter still felt cold under her bare skin, but now it was a relief from the fever inside her. She rocked to him each time their bodies met, rewarded by a slow roll of his hips to give her the sweet friction she so desperately needed. Their movements steadily grew in tempo, his thrusts punctuated by quiet groans in her ear.

She clutched at him as she felt herself drawn closer to climax, not wanting it to end so soon. If this was all she could have of him, it had to last. She had to get her fill while she could, even if part of her worried that there was no such thing as enough of Jackson DeMatteo. Nothing could stop the mounting pleasure inside of her, no matter how much she wanted to draw it out. She cried out his name and arched into him before shuddering in a still, quiet moment of release.

He pulled her closer to him and only then did his thrusts lose their rhythm, coming in unsteady speed until he buried himself inside her with one last groan. Both spent, they panted against the counter. Darla bowed her head over his shoulder, soaking up the sensation of his naked skin against hers.

He turned his head to kiss her. "Come to bed with me?"

Half a dozen reasons to say no were on the tip of her tongue. She had rounds in the morning. What they were doing together could cause so many complications. She was afraid of just how far she'd fall if she slept in his bed. There was only one reason she could think of to say yes.

"All right."

Foolish as it was, she wanted to be there.

Chapter Fifteen

Dreams of broken glass and blood on a sidewalk dragged Jackson down like drowning in tar. When he finally fought his way free, one hand automatically reached for the other side of the bed and found it empty. He rubbed the sleep from his eyes and looked around, half-wondering if Darla had been a dream as well. The indent on the pillow beside his reassured him that it had been very real.

But had it been right? If he went to Singh and told him, she'd almost certainly be transferred. If she wasn't kept out of trauma entirely, then at the very least she wouldn't be allowed to work with him ever again. A vague sense of unease settled in his stomach.

He pulled on a pair of boxers and headed upstairs. Darla had made herself at home at his dining room table, wearing the T-shirt from last night and digging into a carton of ice cream. He checked toward the kitchen and couldn't see the rest of their clothes scattered around. It sounded like she had the washer and dryer both going.

He took a chair next to hers and allowed himself a moment to admire her. With her hair all wild from sleep and sex and in nothing but his T-shirt, he couldn't imagine a sexier image to wake up to. "Chocolate potato chip ice cream for breakfast? Is that healthy?"

She drew her shoulders up a little as her cheeks reddened with embarrassment. "You're the one who had it in his freezer. It was all I could find, other than some nasty looking leftovers."

"I have it for snacking. Not breakfast." He stole the spoon from her for a bite, then snaked an arm around her waist to tug her over into his lap. "And getting such a weird flavor usually saves me from having to share."

He could feel her relaxing again as she settled into his lap, her arms looped loosely around his neck. "Well, you're screwed now, because this happens to be my favorite flavor."

"Damn. I'm in trouble."

Healthy or not, he had to admit that sharing an ice cream breakfast with her was the nicest morning he'd had in years. Which only made things that much harder. If he was honest, that deal with Singh would be out at the very least. A one-time mistake they never spoke of might be safer for the both of them, but the thought didn't provide any comfort.

He took a deep breath to try to prepare himself for some serious, and likely unpleasant, talk. Before he could start, his phone began to ring. He looked around, trying to remember where he'd put it.

Darla slipped off his lap, grabbed it from the counter, and handed it to him. "You left it in your pocket last night and you got some gas on your clothes, too. It's all in the wash."

"Thanks." He looked at the caller ID with a frown before answering it. "Hi Dad. What's going on?"

"Your mom and I wanted to wish you a belated happy birthday." The older DeMatteo's voice didn't sound cheerful enough for birthday wishes. This was the same tone Jackson recalled teaching him geometry.

"Thanks. How are you two doing?"

He braced himself, knowing exactly how that question would be answered. True to form, his father launched into lengthy, dull stories about fixing a fence on their property line and how road construction had forced him into a detour through a part of Kansas City he hated during his morning commute. None of it was personal and, in truth, none of it was even interesting enough for Jackson to keep track of. Boredom tended to dominate his thoughts every time they had one of these stilted conversations, followed by regret and longing for real connection.

When there was a gap in his dad's updates, he sought something neutral to say. Something that could conceivably sound like he'd been listening. "Seems like you're both really busy."

"And what about you? Eliza said you might be getting on the tenure track."

"In theory." He looked toward Darla, who was putting the ice cream back in the freezer. Guilt settled over him. "I'm trying to get the chief's recommendation, but he doesn't make the decision on his own and my competition is pretty good at politics."

"You never should have taken an adjunct position to start with. Begin as you intend to proceed. If you don't start on the right path, it's far too hard to change tracks later down the road."

The mixed metaphors were nearly dizzying. Thank God his father wasn't a literature professor. "I took what I needed to take. It's pretty much impossible to start out a full professor these days."

"And just as close to impossible to switch from adjunct to tenure track. You sabotaged yourself."

He rubbed the worry wrinkle between his eyes with his palm, as if he could physically push the irritation away. "Thanks Dad. I'm really proud of myself and all I've accomplished, too."

"Don't be like that, Jackson. You know we're proud of you. That doesn't mean we're blind to your mistakes."

Of course they weren't. No one was and they'd never let him forget it either. "I have to go."

Darla looked startled by the sound of his phone slapping down on the table. "Wow. That makes me really happy my mom and I get along."

"My dad has a hard time grasping that my career isn't his. He tries to control everything." And instead of growing immune to it, Jackson still found himself hoping things would change. He couldn't decide if he was more annoyed with his father or himself. Seriously, he was a grown-ass adult at the top of his game. Wanting his parents' approval, that was so…puerile.

"My mom's a little controlling too," Darla said. "I think she's just trying to be helpful, though. Maybe that's all your dad is doing."

Her mother was controlling? That gave him pause and he rolled the thought over slowly in his mind. If it was true, it made her comments in surgery to Nancy make more sense. Her mother wanted her to go into trauma and so her own interests didn't matter. "Sometimes parents help us the wrong way."

"I guess that's possible. Or help us more than we really want."

"Come here." He pulled her down back into his lap and nuzzled into the side of her neck, her ebony curls blocking out the rest of the world like a curtain. "You really were amazing last night."

She squirmed in his lap. "Well, I do have a yoga video I follow twice a week."

He laughed, tightening his arms around her, and gave her a quick kiss. "Oh, you were beyond amazing in bed. But I was talking about that little boy."

"I just did what had to be done." One of her hands rested on his chest, and he felt her fingers start to trace over the muscles there. Taking her back to bed was so much more inviting than going to work.

"If trauma is really what you want to specialize in, I think you're going to be a very good surgeon."

Her brows raised a bit and she gave him a smile. "Thank you."

"But." It was the last word he wanted to say. It could only make his deal with Singh harder, yet what kind of man would he be if he kept it to himself? "You could be better than good. I think you could be great if you went into pediatrics."

All the wriggling in his lap and touching stopped instantly. The temperature in the room seemed to drop a few degrees. "Why? Because I'm a woman? Because you figure

I've got to be all nurturing?"

"No. Because you, as an individual, are really good with them. Like Dr. White said, kids aren't just little adults. They have their own unique needs and you handle that well."

She shook her head. "This is what I've been working toward my whole life."

"Okay." Her reaction made the rest of what they needed to talk about harder. White had been right about her talent, but the night between them would cast any of his professional recommendations in a self-serving light, no matter how sincere they were. "You know if we're involved in any way, we're not supposed to be working together like this."

She didn't say anything at first, her expression distant. "It'll be fine."

"I don't think it will be."

She abruptly stood up from his lap and gave him a small, sad smile. "I want to leave at the end of my first year, to transfer back to a hospital in Chicago. Just don't tell anyone before then and it'll be fine, like I said."

Numbness washed over him as her words sank in. It solved the problem, but not in a way he liked. There'd been no hint from Singh that she might leave the hospital. "Does anybody know you're leaving yet?"

"No. I didn't want to talk to the residency program director until after I took my Step Three exam."

So she'd be licensed to practice medicine without supervision, he realized. It'd give her more leverage if anyone was unhappy with her leaving instead of finishing her residency at UMC. He closed his eyes, fighting back his own hurt over how temporary their relationship would be. "When's your Step Three?"

"A couple of weeks away still. My mom's flying out the same day as McGaffey's retirement party next week to help me prepare." She squeezed his shoulder. "I'm going to check my clothes."

McGaffey's position would be filled before she left. It wouldn't interfere with his deal with Singh, but that was a distant concern in comparison to her actually leaving. He rubbed a hand over his face and took a deep breath. *Every relationship has an expiration date*, he reminded himself. This time he was lucky enough to know when it was.

"Are you okay?"

He looked up to see she'd come back, now dressed in her clothes from the night before. Darla's eyes narrowed slightly, looking him over in concern.

"A little disappointed, but I'll be fine. Why?"

She fiddled with the hem of her skirt, chewing on her bottom lip. "The accident last night. I know you said it was just because all the bad driving here makes you angry, but you were mumbling in your sleep and thrashing around like…well. It just seems like you're not fine."

Perceptive of her. The accident probably had at least a little to do with his agitation too. He dragged a hand through his hair, nodding. "I lost someone in a car accident."

She winced, but didn't look at all surprised. "I'm sorry. If you want to talk about it, I'll listen."

Did he want to talk about it? He'd hardly said a word about it to his best friend since the funeral, and he was practically spitting nails every time someone alluded to it at the hospital. But Darla didn't look judgmental, and there was no pity in her eyes. The woman was a master at balancing empathy, it seemed.

"The first year of my residency I had a girlfriend named Amy. She struggled a lot with bipolar disorder and her meds never seemed to work well enough for her. She'd tried to kill herself once that I know about. But she was wonderful. Brilliant and sweet and intuitive." He closed his eyes for a moment, feeling all the pain come back again. "And then…I don't know what happened. She went wandering late one night. Was she having a manic episode? Needed a walk to clear her head? Was it something I did? I'll never get to know, because some drunk hit her in a crosswalk."

"Not having any answers must have been really hard for you."

He nodded slightly. "That's part of it. And the guilt because I couldn't fix everything for her. I couldn't make anything better." He got to his feet abruptly. "I need to get dressed for work. Do you want to get coffee on the way? Maybe a breakfast sandwich?"

She gave him a wan smile. "I wish I could do coffee. I'm going to be a zombie all day."

"You're doing rounds with me. I'll steer you away from neuro so you don't munch brains." He forced himself to grin, even as what she'd said nagged him. She'd mentioned medication the night before and had taken something at dinner. "Why can't you do coffee?"

"Um." A long moment dragged out before she followed that single syllable with more. "I'm on beta-blockers for a mitral valve prolapse and anxiety. Even that chocolate I just had can make things worse for me sometimes, but I still cheat."

Cold fear shot down his spine. So soon after talking about Amy's death, it was hard to shake the chill. "Is it serious?

Didn't you say your dad died from a heart condition?"

"A much more serious one, and it wasn't diagnosed before he died." She said the words in a rush, as if she'd had to make the same reassurance before. "I'm very careful. The anxiety and not being able to chug caffeine are my biggest problems."

He nodded reluctantly. "I guess they would be." He thought back to their first meeting, how he found her in the supply closet—and hated himself for it.

"I'm fine, Jackson," she insisted.

She *did* seem to have things under control. Plenty of people lived long and healthy lives with a minor heart condition like that without being diagnosed at all. But how many of those people were surgical interns, straining their bodies with poor diets and a chronic lack of sleep?

Chapter Sixteen

The sheer agony of life without caffeine didn't fully hit Darla until she tried balancing a love life with sixteen-hour workdays. Getting home again after her shift and crawling into bed was all a blur. So was showering and eating and getting dressed the next day.

Brandon watched her with his brow furrowed in concern as she got out of his car in the employee parking lot at the hospital. "I'm starting to see why you hate those beta-blockers."

"It actually hasn't been as bad as I worried it'd be. If I'm getting enough sleep, anyway. The list of stuff I'm not supposed to eat sucks a little. Processed sugar, chocolate, alcohol…"

"How can you even live like that?"

She rolled her eyes. "It's not that bad, and I don't always stick to it. The lack of constant migraines and anxiety attacks makes it all worthwhile."

"Okay, so. I've got a question. If adrenaline is bad for you and you need to do all this stuff to keep your heart from going too fast—"

"I can exercise," she interrupted. "I've got to be careful with it and I do get out of breath no matter how much I train, but it's good for me. My cardiologist recommends it even."

Brandon shook his head with an annoyed expression. "I know you jog. I meant, how do you have sex?"

"Oh God, Brandon." She covered her face with one hand. "I'm not answering that. If you know what's good for you, you're never going to ask it again. Ever."

"It's just healthy medical curiosity."

She dropped her hand to glare at him. "It's as gross and wrong as me asking you how *you* have sex."

Brandon's question coupled with the knowledge she'd be on Jackson's service again made it difficult to keep her mind on work. Delicious memories of being in Jackson's bed kept creeping back in, overshadowed only by the memories of being on Jackson's counter. If she closed her eyes, she swore she could retrace every spot where his fingers had slid on her skin, as if they'd burned themselves into her flesh.

Ten minutes later, she was in her scrubs and ready to report for rounds. She stepped into the elevator and hit the button for her floor.

"Can you hold that for us?" a voice called.

Automatically, she put her hand out to keep the doors opened. Only then did she notice who had spoken. A man in an all-black costume with a bat-eared cowl was walking toward her, flanked by several other superheroes.

If glee was light, Darla was sure her smile would have been blinding. She looked over the group as they stepped into the elevator, then out past them into the lobby they'd just left. A few of the staff were doing their best not to stare, but others were smiling and talking about the spectacle.

"Dr. White called you? That's fantastic."

"You know Nancy?" a woman with a yellow cape asked.

"I've worked with her a little. I actually told her about you guys and how I thought it'd be good for the kids."

"Thanks for the recommendation." The woman beamed. "We always love going somewhere new. Most of the time, we're over at St. Jude's Ranch."

The doors slid open again. Before them stood Jackson and Nancy, who looked to have been deep in conversation. Jackson just barely turned his head to the side to acknowledge Darla's arrival, then did a double-take.

"What is that?" he asked.

"The volunteer group for patient morale." Nancy clapped him on the shoulder and smiled to Darla. "It was her idea."

Darla moved closer to him as they dispersed from the elevator. Even without any caffeine, she could feel nerves bubbling up inside of her like a Coke sent on a roller-coaster. "I told you about cosplay."

"Yeah, you did, I just..." He trailed off, staring at one of the men in the group as he pulled on a Spider-Man hood. "I think I misunderstood what cosplay is."

"The kids really love it. They get to meet their heroes and have this great experience to take them away from their fear and pain, you know?"

"That's sweet." Jackson tore his gaze away from the costumed volunteers to refocus on Darla. The shock in his jade green eyes gave way to something warmer and softer, instantly melting away her tension. "And a really good idea. Maybe you should request Dr. White's service more often."

She stepped a little closer to him, lowering her voice. "But I like working with you."

One of his hands skimmed her arm, sending shivers racing down her spine. It could easily have just been a friendly touch, but there was no convincing her body of that now. "I like working with you, too, but you seem awfully drawn to pediatrics."

She took a deep breath to try to center herself, but all it accomplished was heightening her awareness of his scent. His earthy cologne and the mouth-wateringly masculine scent of his clean skin itself were nearly enough to make her forget where she was. "Liking kids isn't the same as being good at pediatric surgery."

He came closer, his lips hovering beside her ear so his breath tickled. "I know talent when I see it. Just accept that."

"Okay," she whispered.

Behind Jackson, an unwelcome, mocking voice spoke up. "Trying to screw your intern into submission, DeMatteo?"

The moment shattered, leaving her cold, muscles tense. She jerked free of Jackson's touch and looked up to see another doctor watching them. Mevlyn again. Another trauma surgeon, though not one she'd ever worked with. Between this and the last conversation she'd had with him, she was now grateful for that.

A muscle was jumping in Jackson's cheek as he ground his teeth together, not turning to face the other man. "Morning, Dick. What can I help you with?" His voice was tight in contrast to the pleasant words.

"I'm a little concerned about a lack of professionalism

here. You're supposed to be educating her, you know. Not getting into her panties."

Anger flared in Jackson's eyes, sudden enough to make her take a step backwards in shock. This time he did turn away from Darla to face Mevlyn. "Don't talk about Morales that way ever again."

"Then don't give me anything to talk about. I thought you two were looking a little too close."

"Shut up." The words came out as nearly a growl, his hands curling into fists. "Don't say another word about it."

"About what?" Mevlyn screwed up his face as though he were thinking, then smirked at Darla, ignoring Jackson for the moment. "That you need her for Singh's recommendation?"

Jackson stepped forward as if to grab onto Mevlyn. What he'd intended to do next, Darla couldn't know, because instead Mevlyn jerked backwards and slammed into the young man in the Spicer-Man costume, knocking him into the wall.

"Excuse me!" He pushed Mevlyn off of him.

Mevlyn shook his head slowly, his upper lip curled with disgust, and walked away.

Darla put a hand over her chest, the pounding of her heart vibrating beneath her palm. "What the hell was that about?"

"Dick being Dick. It's nothing." Jackson stepped over to the young man Mevlyn had bumped into, checking to make sure he was all right.

All Darla could do was watch. What did she have to do with the Chief of Trauma Medicine giving Jackson a recommendation? She assumed it had something to do with the professorship position he wanted. Something that made

Jackson defensive. She watched him with narrowed eyes, suspicion getting the better of her.

Once the cosplayers had gone on their way and it was clear no harm had been done, Jackson turned back to her. "Come on. We're already running late on rounds."

She followed him, but her concerns wouldn't stop nagging at her. "Were you talking to me about pediatrics the other morning to help your career? So I won't be on your service?"

"Excuse me?" The look he gave her was full of such naked bafflement she had to believe it was sincere. "No, I'm not. Believe me, that's about the last thing that would help my career."

"Then what is it?"

"It's complicated. Maybe we could get into it after work, but right now isn't the best time."

"Fine."

Jackson paused outside a patient's room to check the chart. While he was reading it, a nurse approached with a worried expression on his face.

"Dr. DeMatteo? Chief Singh needs to see you in his office."

Jackson frowned and didn't look away from the chart. "Can it wait?"

"I'm afraid not."

He sighed and handed the tablet to Darla. "Monitor my patients and let them know I'll be with you as soon as I can."

Chapter Seventeen

The sight of Dr. Richard Mevlyn sitting in Singh's office made Jackson's stomach burn with acid. His hand gripped the doorknob tight enough to make his knuckles ache, which seemed a better option than busting those same knuckles on Dick's smug face.

"Shut the door, DeMatteo." Singh looked like he'd just taken a bite off a lemon. "It's bad enough the two of you fought in the hallway like a couple of junior high students."

He started it. Jackson bit his tongue to keep from reinforcing the chief's view of them as children. He shut the door behind him, then took the empty chair.

Singh leaned back, hands steepled before him. "What's this about?"

Dick jutted his jaw forward as he spoke, the picture of righteous indignation. "He was flirting with an intern. Morales. I confronted him about his behavior, and he threatened to hit me."

"I didn't threaten anything." Jackson rolled his eyes. "I was *going* to hit you and then you tripped into someone instead."

Singh pinched the bridge of his nose, his forehead wrinkled up like a cheap suit. "You can't hit people at work, DeMatteo."

Jackson leaned back in his chair, fingers drumming on one armrest. Warnings were going off in his head not to push things, not to be too aggressive or defensive, but that self-protection warred with honor. Even as he worried about the consequences, he was gratified to let honor win. "You can't sexually harass interns either."

Singh gave him a hard look. "What are you talking about?"

"A hostile workplace." He jerked a thumb toward Dick. "He was harassing her, talking about screwing her and getting into her panties."

Dick went stiff in his chair, leaning forward. "Whoa, hey. You're taking that out of context."

"Yeah? The context of using your position to publicly humiliate and intimidate an intern?"

"Enough." Singh shook his head at the two of them, his lips pressed into a thin line. "You can't mentor a resident you're dating, DeMatteo."

Darla had asked him not to tell anyone. Did that mean he had to lie, too? This was all getting rapidly out of control. After a litany of swearing in his head, he nodded. "I know. I'm not." Even as he said it, he knew that somehow, someway, this was going to bite him in the ass.

"Good. And for God's sake, you can't punch your co-workers, even if they are being asses."

Dick sputtered. "That's not fair."

"I don't care if it's fair or not. I care about providing a safe working environment and avoiding lawsuits. What were you thinking, Mevlyn?"

"Come on. I didn't mean it seriously. I wasn't trying to hit on her or something."

Singh rose from his chair and gestured toward the door. "'Hitting on' someone isn't the problem here. Please, both of you, no more of this. If you act like children again, I won't hesitate to fire you."

Jackson's mood remained foul for the rest of the day, a fact he was sure Darla had picked up on but he avoided answering her questions. Lying for her had been his own decision, but talking about it while he was still upset carried the risk of making her feel blamed. There was little chance to cool off enough to explain it to her when the threat of being fired hung over his head no matter what he did to try to keep his mind off of it. He wanted nothing more than to take Darla home and forget about the world for a few hours, but even that was denied him. She was scheduled for an overnight float, staying in the hospital all night to keep an eye on patients and be available in case of an emergency.

He went home, showered, changed, and then realized the futility of it all and went back to the hospital.

It took a few minutes before she could respond to his text messages, then followed his directions to one of the on-call rooms. Equipped with bunk beds and a table, they gave doctors somewhere to rest when it was desperately needed.

Darla shut the door, her smile threatening to split her

face. "I'd been worrying you were mad at me."

"I'm not mad at you." He shook his head a little and pulled a salad out of the bag he'd brought. "I couldn't sleep at home, and I figured you might want something to eat that didn't come from the cafeteria."

"Thanks." She sat and took a few bites off the salad with such desperation he wondered if she'd stopped to eat anything all day. She washed the salad down with the juice he'd brought her, then sighed. "Working overnight like this is the worst. I don't know how I'll survive my second year."

"Yeah, the twenty-eight hour shifts second year are brutal." Even with caffeine, he recalled. He wondered just how literal her struggle to survive her second year would be. Something calmer and slower sounded so much safer for her.

He leaned back from the table, watching her and thinking. Part of him still couldn't quite believe Singh's threat, but he'd never known the Chief of Trauma Medicine to bluff.

The obvious answer to avoiding any further problems was right in front of him, but it made him sick to consider.

He spun the cap from his own bottle of juice on the table, watching it roll instead of looking at her. Every time she caught his eye, he could feel his brain shutting down and all he wanted to do was touch her. "I'm sorry for upsetting you the other morning, when I said you should switch to pediatrics."

"It's okay. I probably overreacted." She shrugged. "My mom's dealt with a lot of racism and sexism over the years from trauma surgeons, and taking care of kids seems like such a girly thing to do."

"What's wrong with girly?" He spun the bottle cap again, flicking it toward her.

She caught the cap before it spun off the edge of the table and gave him a confused look. "What do you mean?"

"You're very feminine, very nurturing, very sweet. Why do you have a problem embracing your strengths?"

"I'm not..." She trailed off, shaking her head. "Being a woman doesn't mean I have to be a pediatrician."

"McGaffey is probably the best trauma surgeon in this hospital, and she's a woman." He took a sip off his juice, wishing it was something harder. "When I suggested pediatrics to you, it really was just because I thought you'd be good at it. Nothing more to it than that." Though now he found himself wishing she'd switch to it for entirely different reasons.

"Do you know how often male doctors are telling female med students and residents that they should do 'girly' medicine? Maybe you didn't mean anything by it, but there's a context to it all, Jackson." She stood up to throw away her salad bowl and bottle.

He followed behind her, wrapping his arms around her waist before she could turn around. She relaxed back into him, her generously curved body fitting as if there was nowhere else she was ever meant to be. Need for her gnawed at him now that he was finally touching her again. He brushed the side of her neck with a kiss.

"I guess I didn't think about that. I'm sorry." He nuzzled into her hair and inhaled her scent deeply. How could she work grueling hours in a hospital day and night and yet still smell so sweet? "You follow your heart and don't worry about whatever stupid thing I say. If this is what you want, then go for it. If you want it, you could eventually take McGaffey's spot as the best here."

He expected her to react warmly to the compliment, not stiffen in his arms as if he'd just said something horrible. "Jackson." Her voice was tight around his name, maybe even holding back tears.

He released her, remembering why she wouldn't ever take McGaffey's spot. It'd be someone else she'd be measuring up to in Chicago. "Right. I forgot."

She parted her lips like she was going to answer him, then stepped forward to catch him in a kiss. To his surprise, she clung to him with breathless passion, as if it were the last time they'd ever kiss at all. If a picture could speak a thousand words, then the soft strokes of lips on lips could speak volumes. He ached to lose himself in her and let common sense fall away, but not even her soft body against him could make him forget that meeting with Singh.

Outside in the hall, voices grew louder as they came closer.

"Do you know where Morales went?"

"I think a friend brought her food and she was going to eat and nap in an on-call room. Do you need her?"

The voices continued on, growing quieter again, but the reminder was enough.

Jackson jerked back from the kiss, then ran his fingers through his hair to smooth it back into place.

"I need to go."

"Are you sure? I've got more time to—"

He shook his head and grabbed the doorknob. "Good night." He shut the door behind him again while his self-preservation was stronger than the hurt look in Darla's eyes.

Chapter Eighteen

As tiring as working overnight was, the time off afterwards to catch up on her sleep had almost been worth it. All that time lazing in bed would have been even better if Darla could have shared some of it with Jackson, but he was working for most of it and never responded to her calls later in the day.

The lack of word from him bugged her, especially after the way he'd run off from the on-call room. With her United States Medical Licensing Examination Step Three looming and her mother due to arrive the next day, she did her best not to dwell on it.

She was just finishing up some of her administrative hours at the hospital when Maggie stopped and pointed a finger dramatically at her. "Okay, give me pseudo-gout associations."

Darla grinned. With their Step Three exam looming, they'd been bouncing their flashcards off of one another every chance they got. Except never while eating, by mutual agreement. "Hemochromatosis, hyperparathyroidism, acromegaly, and hypothyroidism. Now give me five causes of microcytic anemia."

Maggie pursed her lips and was quiet for a moment before answering. "Iron deficiency, lead poisoning, anemia of chronic disease, thalassemia, and sideroblastic anemia."

"You got it."

"Woo! So did you." Maggie high-fived her. "Medical licenses, here we come."

"It's still pretty weird to think that we're almost there. We'll still have years on our specialties, but..." Jackson walked towards her. Darla smiled, hoping whatever had bothered him before was done.

The look on his face when he saw her was difficult to read. His eyes lingered too long for simple polite interest, then tried to avoid her entirely as if he weren't aware she was there. Before she could think about it enough to worry, Darla stepped away from the desk and Maggie.

"I'll see you later," she called over her shoulder, then closed the distance between herself and Jackson. "I need to talk to you."

His eyes remained locked straight ahead. "I'm really busy right now. Can it wait?"

It had already waited too long as far as Darla was concerned. She looked around, spotting the supply closet she had hidden in during her panic attack the first day she worked with him. She closed her fingers around his arm and dragged him toward the door, expecting some sort of resistance from him. Instead, despite his verbal protests and refusal to look at her, he went with her so easily it might as well have been his suggestion.

She shut the door behind them, then leaned against it to block his escape. "Why are you avoiding me?"

Finally, his eyes met hers. The muscles in his jaw were visibly tense. "I had to lie and say we weren't seeing each other. Then the chief threatened to fire me over that scene with Mevlyn the other day."

Fired? That sounded drastic. Guilt twisted her stomach into knots, and she wondered just how much of the situation rested squarely on her shoulders. "If you called me when you went home, we wouldn't have had to talk about this in the hospital."

"Yeah, I know, but what we're doing is making me question my judgment with you. I can't help you learn if I'm second-guessing myself every step of the way because of what's happening here."

"And what's happening?"

He brought his hand up to cup her cheek instead of answering and her eyes closed of their own volition as she leaned into his touch. It wasn't fair at all that he had this kind of power over her. His other hand went to the small of her back to draw her closer and she felt the warmth of his lips and breath just inches from her ear.

"Complete and utter loss of control. When you're around, all I can think about is you." He kissed in the little hollow where her ear and jaw met, making her shiver. "You're my kryptonite."

Already she could feel her frustration evaporating, replaced with the heat spreading through her veins at his touch. She turned her face toward him, her lips barely glancing over his before she murmured. "See, you do have a little bit of geek in you."

He laughed and kissed her bottom lip before giving it a small tug that made her hiss. "You're a bad influence on me."

"I'm not sorry." Hadn't getting under his skin been her goal all along? All right, true, she hadn't planned on doing it by hopping into bed with him, but pushing him to live a little certainly felt like an accomplishment. "You needed to get that stick out of your ass."

He pressed closer to her until she was trapped between his body and the door, a fate she couldn't possibly complain about. The heat of his growing arousal was hot against her hip, weakening her knees until she was sure it was only his body keeping her upright.

"We really can't keep doing this. It'll cause problems."

She licked her lips and rolled forward to work herself against him, rewarded with a strangled groan low in his throat. Her lips stroked over his again, her tongue just barely teasing at his bottom lip to catch a taste of him. "Who're you trying to convince?"

Her name was almost a growl on his breath before he crushed his mouth to hers. All the passion and feeling he kept bottled up inside of him nearly overwhelmed her as he unleashed it in the kiss, plundering her mouth as if his life depended on it. It was easy to be swept away with it, too easy. Her body was buzzing with need, but there was more to it than just need for his body.

She broke the kiss first, turning her head slightly to the side. He took it as an invitation to trail his lips down the side of her neck, drawing whimpers from her. Maybe for once her anxiety was working in her favor, as it kept nagging at her to think straight.

"You can't ignore me." The words were barely more than a whisper when she first got them out. She cleared her throat, then tried again. "I'm not some mistake you can feel bad about and avoid. I'm a person. You want me, you deal with me. Even the complicated bits."

He pulled back from her, green eyes now dark with hunger. Several tense heartbeats passed before he nodded. "No more avoiding you."

"Thank you." She slid a hand up the back of his neck to bury in his dark brown hair, then pulled him in to kiss again. Her other hand went to the front of his slacks, stroking his arousal through the cloth.

He groaned and broke the kiss, his lips trailing across her cheek. "What are you doing?"

"We have some unfinished business from the on-call room."

"The on-call room had beds."

Her hand went still, doubt tugging at her. Maybe it was too much, but he made her feel fearless. "So that's a no?"

"It's just risky. I don't even have a condom with me."

She nodded, then offered tentatively, "I have an IUD?"

His answer was a feral growl. She bit her lip to fight back a delighted laugh at successfully tempting him, which became a quiet, stifled moan when he spun her against the door and then worked a hand down the front of her scrubs. His other hand made short work of their clothes, getting them just enough out of the way so she could feel his hot, naked flesh on hers.

"I don't know how such a smart woman can turn me so stupid," he breathed against her ear.

She reached back to bury her hand in his hair as she

leaned into him, nuzzling his cheek. "That's what smart women are best at."

With a roll of his hips he entered her, making her body ache pleasantly as it stretched around him. The suddenness and risk of the situation added an urgency to every little touch that put her instantly on edge. He thrust slowly at first, giving her a moment to adjust, then began driving into her at a pace that left her breathlessly gasping.

Pinned to the door by his weight and the passion of his movements, she could barely rock to meet him. It left her acutely focused on him and the sensation of each stroke dragging along her inner walls. She wanted to wrap herself up in the warm feel of his arms around her and the earthy scent of his skin, to hold the memory of it with her. There was no future. Only this.

As his thrusts grew shorter, his hand slid down her body. He worked his middle finger over her clit in time with his thrusts, drawing her body tighter with need until she reached the breaking point. Unable to make a sound, she hissed inward through clenched teeth, shivering and rolling between him and the door. He buried his face in the side of her neck a moment later, muffling his groans.

She rested her forehead against the panel, panting. There was something so satisfying about misbehaving with him. "I can't believe we just did that." Darla tugged her clothes back into place and turned around to watch Jackson doing the same. A soft, giddy laugh escaped her at the absurdity of the situation.

"That was really going above and beyond ignoring Singh's warning." Despite the words, Jackson only looked pleased with himself. He leaned in to kiss her again, his arms sliding around her. "You make me want to break all the rules, Darla. When we're together…it's the only thing that matters."

It would be so easy to just melt into him and forget the entire day, but reality was already worming its way into her head. Worry over how long she'd been gone and if anyone had noticed their departure to the closet together…

"I really do need to go." She kissed his cheek. "I was hoping you'd come over later. I've got to pick my mom up from the airport tomorrow morning, but I'm still free tonight."

He was wearing that frustratingly closed-off expression he used when he was trying to hide his feelings. "I can do that. We're running out of time, aren't we?"

"Yeah, I guess we are."

He gave her a hard kiss, then walked out. Following right after him might be too obvious, so she leaned against the wall to wait. Chicago was sounding worse by the minute, but now it could be the best option to protect him.

Chapter Nineteen

An hour later, Darla still hadn't shaken the feeling of unease. It had started out as fun with Jackson, making her feel good about herself and pulling him out of his self-imposed isolation. With her leaving, it had seemed safe, too. Maybe her feelings were at risk, but nothing else. Now she'd never felt stupider.

She took a deep breath through her nose and let it out slowly, but it did little to release the tension.

Maggie frowned and set down the flashcards on the table in the resident break room. "Are you okay? You're breathing kinda funny."

"Just a little upset. It's nothing."

Her friend looked her up and down with a skeptical eye. "That doesn't look like nothing."

Darla shook her head. "I just did something dumb. It's no big deal."

"I don't care what stupid thing you did. Relax so you

don't have a panic attack, all right?"

"It's not a panic attack." She felt a little off, but knew panic attacks well enough to recognize one when it was starting. She started to check her pulse when her pager went off to summon her to the ambulance bay. "Gotta go."

Each footfall on the run there tightened the tension in her chest until it ached, and her throat burned. She'd nearly made it to the bay when she had to stop and grab onto the wall, her vision swimming with black spots. There was no need to check her pulse now, as she could feel her heart hammering unsteadily.

Her gasping caught the attention of the staff waiting for the ambulance and several of them turned to look at her. Jackson was among them and the alarm on his face told her everything she needed to know about how bad she looked.

"Darla," he started, stepping toward her.

The black spots spread across her vision until everything was blocked out and she felt her knees collapse under her.

Jackson dove forward to catch Darla before she hit her head on the hard floor, but Singh was there before him to catch her under the arms. All it left Jackson to do for the moment was stare in horror. What the hell had happened to her? She wasn't the first resident he'd seen pass out, but that was more likely to happen in the OR than after running to meet an ambulance. Those residents didn't normally have heart conditions, either.

"We need a gurney over here," Singh called.

Outside, the ambulance was arriving. He helped get her

onto the gurney and stepped back, knowing that he had other people to tend to but hating it all the while. "She has a mitral valve prolapse and takes a beta-blocker."

Singh gave a short nod before speaking to a nurse. "Page cardio."

As much as it killed him, he had to step out to meet the ambulance. It was a blessedly low-risk trauma case involving two teenagers and a nail gun, letting him get caught up in the rhythms of treatment with little chance of facing life and death decisions.

"I can understand how one of them got a nail through his hand, but I don't get how they managed to nail themselves together after that," his nurse commented when it was all over.

Jackson shook his head and reached up to pull the surgical cap off. "People can do amazingly stupid things. Page me when ortho is done with his hand."

Running off to try to find out what had happened to Darla as soon as possible wouldn't necessarily look good, but he couldn't bring himself to care under the circumstances.

Singh found him first in the hall, annoyance clear on his face. "If you're looking for Morales, she's being sent home for the day."

He released a heavy breath in relief. "So she's okay?"

"You know I can't discuss that with you."

It was answer enough. If something had been at all questionable, they would have kept her for at least a few hours. Not just enough time for him to pull nails out of a couple of kids. Sending her home was the best possible outcome.

"I saw the look on your face when she fell," Singh went on. "You want to be honest with me this time?"

Relief was swiftly replaced with a sinking sensation. Jackson pinched the bridge of his nose, remembering that little anxiety chant of Darla's the day they'd met. *I hate everyone and everything. Especially me.* He could finally relate to it.

"We've been seeing each other." Not having to lie again was at least some small consolation. "She's planning on leaving at the end of her first year, though. I'm not going to have any long-term influence over her career."

"That's good for next year, DeMatteo, but that doesn't change anything right now."

"So don't let me work with her again then. Hell, don't let me ever work with residents."

Singh shook his head. "No, that's why the subordinate employee gets transferred. You're more valuable. We want you sharing your skills and experience with everyone you can."

At least that didn't sound like he was being fired. Yet. He'd take what small victory he could get. "What are you going to do?"

"I'm not sure yet. We'll discuss it tomorrow at our meeting."

Jackson knocked at Darla's apartment door with his free hand, which had a takeout bag hooked over his fingers. When she opened it, her eyes focused on the bottle and she raised a brow. "I don't know if drinking is a good idea. Especially after the day I had."

"It's sparkling juice. You'll be fine." He leaned in to kiss her cheek, then stepped through the door, hoping his own words were true. "*Are* you okay?"

"Completely."

She looked comfortable, having changed out of her scrubs and into yoga pants. The simple domesticity of it appealed. Her color was good, and she was moving around just fine, but it was difficult to shake his fear entirely as he headed for the kitchen. "I hope you like pad thai."

"It depends. Does it have shrimp in it?"

He tipped the container to show her inside. "Chicken."

"Perfect."

The need to know was gnawing at him. No matter how many times he told himself it was unlikely to be something serious, he couldn't shake the fear. "What happened to you today?"

Darla wrinkled up her nose. "Syncope. You know, the fancy medical way of saying I passed out. My meds had lowered my heart rate too much and then I ran. It made for a bad combination is all. Not much different from standing up too fast, really."

It sounded like it would be a bad combination for the rest of her life if she insisted on working in trauma. And that was just one complication. He'd read about others. Infective endocarditis. Congestive heart failure. Cardiac arrest. Even if they were rare, it was hard to not worry about all the things that could go wrong. He gave her a pained look. "And you're sure you're okay?"

"My pride is the only thing that's been harmed," she assured him.

Once they each had a plate, they sat the kitchen island to eat. He'd spent almost every free moment of the day thinking over what to say to make her stay, but now it all sounded so trite when he replayed it in his head.

"I don't want you to go." There. Direct, simple.

Darla washed her food down with a sip of the grape juice, frowning. "I was kind of hoping you didn't *want* me to go. I'm not sure I'd let you come over if I thought you did."

"I mean I want you to stay."

She looked down at her food for a moment, poking at the rice noodles with her fork. "I never planned on being this far away from home. The resident match didn't include a single Midwestern hospital, so Vegas was the best choice out of all of them."

His heart sank. "I guess you've got a lot of family and friends back there."

"Not really. It's mostly my mom and me. I had other family, but they moved. I lost touch with most of my old friends during med school and all my med school friends are scattered around the country." She sighed and finally raised her eyes from the noodles to meet his. "I hate leaving my mom all alone."

The thought of worrying about his mother in that way and moving across the country for her struck him as foreign. He loved his parents, of course, but hadn't made a single decision with them in mind since he'd turned eighteen.

"Most people move away from their mothers eventually. It's okay."

"I'm not most people. We always had this plan, the two of us. I'd become a trauma surgeon and work at her hospital and we'd kick ass and take names together."

"You know you could do that with her at any hospital. Doesn't sound like she has anything keeping her in Chicago, either."

Darla started to say something in response, then stopped, her mouth forming an adorable O. "I hadn't thought of it like that."

"So think about it. You know lots of people here. You've got me, all your girlfriends, your roommate Brad."

She drew her brows together for a moment before the confusion on her face cleared to be replaced with a smile. "You mean Brandon?"

Shit. At least he hadn't used the wrong name to his face, as far as he could remember. "Yeah, him. You seem happy here."

She tucked her hair back behind her ears, head bowed forward slightly to make it difficult to see her expression. "I am." The words were so soft he nearly missed them.

"So stay."

"For you?"

"In part." Jackson set his fork down to reach out to her and comb his fingers through her curls. Whatever new things she'd started doing with them, he approved. It made it difficult to resist playing with her hair constantly, though.

She leaned into the touch like a cat. "Aren't you still worried about what Singh said and the two of us messing up your career?"

There was no delaying it any longer. "He called me out on lying to him today. I had to tell him the truth. He didn't fire me."

"Crap, Jackson." She sighed heavily. "I'm sorry."

"We'll deal with it." He tried to make his voice sound optimistic, even if he felt anything but. "Don't worry."

"Do you know how silly it is to tell me of all people not to worry?"

He laughed in spite of himself. "Okay, yeah. But I think things will work out all right. If you stay."

She was quiet for a long time, her eyes closed, her head tipped back a little while he played with her hair. It drew his attention to her neck, stretched and inviting his kisses. While he waited for her response, he kissed the smooth column of her throat, then rested his lips over her pulse point. Feeling its steady beat was reassuring.

"Let me think about it." The words were a whisper against his ear, and then she curled in close to him, wrapping her arms around him. "I still worry about the chief and my mom and if this is even a good reason to stay."

Her doubts stung, though there was nothing he could say in response. There was no telling what Singh would decide. Maybe it was healthier for her to go back to Chicago and have her mother nearby. The deal with Singh was obviously moot now, but he'd still never explained it to her. Would she stay if she knew? He couldn't envision it, nor could he blame her for leaving. The ethical choice was so clear it might as well have been in neon letters on the wall.

Later, he decided. He'd be completely honest, eventually. He just needed a little more time with her first.

Jackson caught her in a kiss to silence any more of her fears and his own thoughts. As he slid off his stool, he pulled her up into his arms and off her seat, making her squeak in shock. He laughed at the undignified sound and gave her another quick kiss. "Do you mind?"

She looped her arms around his neck and leaned back to give him a narrow-eyed look, though it didn't stop her lips from curling up in a playful smile. "I don't know. Where are you taking me?"

"I was thinking the bed."

"The bed?" She gasped and widened her eyes. "That's pretty kinky. I don't know if I'm ready for a bed."

"The best way to find out is by trying it."

Chapter Twenty

Darla's bedroom was as modest as the rest of the apartment, completely dominated by the bed that took up most of the small floor plan. It only took Jackson two steps from the door—which he kicked shut—before he laid her back on the bed and climbed on top of her.

Laughing, she pulled him down closer to catch him in a brief kiss. "You really do love to be in control, don't you?"

He drew back a little to give her a puzzled look, brows drawn together. "What do you mean?"

"Picking me up. Carrying me around like a Viking with his conquest." She pushed his chest to make him roll over onto his back, then straddled his hips. He was beautiful from every angle she'd ever seen him from, but she had to admit that him lying on her bed was an especially nice view.

"I thought you liked that."

"I do, but…" Her lips brushed over his softly. One of his hands moved up into her hair to pull her into the kiss and she felt his lips part under hers to deepen it. Rather than give in, she pulled back and grinned. "I'd like to do some exploring of my own."

"Exploring?" His eyes darted off to the side as if searching for something and he frowned. "What do you mean?"

She slid her hands between them to push his shirt up. "Your body."

His pale green eyes darkened with hunger, and she felt his hand tighten its grip on her hip. "I wouldn't complain about that."

She tugged his shirt up and over his head, then dropped it beside them on the bed. As soon as it was off, he wrapped his arms around her again, but she wasn't done yet. Leaning into him, her hands slid lower to start at his belt. Her lips brushed against his again, then pressed more firmly as she deepened the kiss. This time he let her take control. She sighed into the kiss as her tongue slid past his lips, first tracing over his teeth before seeking out his tongue with hers. He responded warmly to the kiss, but didn't try to take control, though she could tell by the tension in his body that it was difficult for him.

Once she had his jeans open, her hand slipped inside his boxers to stroke him. He felt thick and heavy, and she marveled that he could be so gentle. Her fingers slid along his shaft slowly, wanting to memorize every inch of him. If she stayed, she'd have more than memories, though. The thought filled her with a warm glow. Soon, she couldn't stand it any longer and broke the kiss with a quiet gasp. Her eyes moved over his chest and stomach, then lower to admire him.

"I don't know how you manage to be so beautiful."

Using the tip of her tongue, she traced the lines of muscle

on his chest, just as she'd been wanting to do since the first time she saw him shirtless. His response was a soft moan, his hand entangling in her hair. She dragged her tongue over his nipple and then breathed against the flat oval. He shivered and goosebumps rose on his skin, making her grin. She repeated the tease on his other nipple, then continued lower. His body was pure masculine perfection. His stomach taut with gentle ripples of muscle visible through the skin. Her favorite part of his bare torso was the V of muscle on his abdomen that narrowed down between his hips, like a natural frame for the rock hard shaft there.

Her tongue followed one side of that muscle, moving downward and inward until she reached the dark brown hair at the base of his shaft. She nuzzled into it, then shifted her grip on his arousal so she could kiss her way up its side uninterrupted.

She brushed her lips against the ridge of his head, then kissed lightly at the tip. He made a quiet sound low in his throat. His eyes were narrowed, watching everything she did with a level of need she had never seen on his face before. The tip of her tongue teased at his crown, tasting the salt of his skin, before she closed her lips around him to draw him deep into her mouth.

The reaction was wonderful. His hips rolled off the bed, his hands gripping the bedspread, and he groaned as his head fell back. His eyes closed for a moment before, with what looked like a great deal of effort, he opened them to watch her again.

As she continued to tease him, the small, involuntary movements of his hips and his quiet moans guided her. "I think I like you exploring." Her belly tightened at the raw need in his voice.

She concentrated on what she was doing. There was something truly amazing in worshiping his body, knowing that he was enjoying everything she did as she reveled in him. Being the entire focus of his attention and hunger made her feel more desirable than she had ever felt in her life. Gorgeous as he was, he wanted *her*. Not just for a handful of nights, but enough to ask her to stay. So many doors for the future were open now, and she didn't know what to do with them.

"Stop, Darla." He sounded breathless and his fingers combed through her hair to gently nudge her back. "There's a lot more I want to do before I'm done tonight."

"What is it you want?"

He immediately kicked off his shoes, then moved to remove the last of his clothing. Once he was nude, he sat up on his knees and cupped her cheek in his hand. "You."

His lips found hers again, making her sigh and lean into him. His arms moved around her to stroke over her back, then down lower to get underneath her yoga pants. Both hands gripped the full curves of her ass, tugging her close. The kiss left her breathless and reeling. Just when she thought she couldn't take it any longer, he broke it off. His silky soft lips slid over her throat, before he nuzzled and she felt the scrape of stubble there. It was followed a moment later by his teeth nibbling over her pulse.

"Please, Jackson."

His lips gently pressed a kiss at the hollow of her throat. "What?"

"I want you."

He released her to tug her shirt over her head. He shifted

to take control and stopped himself. "This is supposed to be about you exploring me, isn't it? So how do you want me? Whatever you want tonight."

She stripped out of her remaining clothes before she pushed him back onto the bed.

"I like you like this." She grinned down at him, noting the way he watched her like she might disappear at any moment. *It doesn't have to end*, she reminded herself. They could have countless nights together if she stayed.

"I like you this way too."

Before she could dwell on it any further, his lips were on hers again, hungrily claiming her. He cupped her breast, massaging the soft mound. The other hand slid over her stomach and then she felt his fingers teasing there before sliding lower. They stroked at her slick folds, making her whimper into the kiss. Just the promise of being with him was enough to arouse her, but touching him had been as much of a sweet torment for her as it had been for him. His fingers slid back and forth, pressing between her lips. One finger lightly circled her clit and her hips automatically jerked forward at the touch.

She didn't want to stop—*God, the man had masterful hands*—but his willingness to relinquish control was too great an opportunity to ignore.

As she lowered herself and felt the heat of his shaft sliding into her, she sighed his name and rolled her hips. His arms wrapped her closer, driving him deeper inside her. On the next stroke they found a rhythm together, as perfect as it ever felt with him, but there were so many possibilities now. Jackson held her tighter, kissed her until she was breathless, and every time he drew back from her lips she opened her eyes to see him watching her raptly.

Soon he wasn't the only one clinging desperately, trying to stretch every second into hours. She kissed his ear, the side of his neck, and along his shoulder, stroking at his skin with her lips to claim every inch of him. Whatever happened, they still had this night, and she intended to make good use of it, but how could she seriously consider walking away? Everything felt too good, too right.

His lips took hers again, and she melted into the kiss, trying to draw comfort from it to chase away the gloom. Their movements together grew faster until his arms tightened around her, pinning her to his chest, and he rolled to pin her beneath him. She watched him through heavy-lidded eyes. With the way he reverently touched her everywhere at once, she would have thought it was his last night on earth.

Nothing could last forever, no matter how badly they tried to draw it out. She rolled up to him with a gasp and then froze there, muscles fluttering and lights flashing behind her eyes. She was dimly aware of his thrusts coming faster and deeper, until he buried himself in her with a groan, clutching her to his chest.

A minute or two passed as she laid there, listening to her hammering pulse and feeling the room spin around her. When she could breathe steadily again, she turned to kiss his cheek and breathe in the welcome, clean musk of his skin. He made a soft sound before rolling onto his side next to her. He wrapped an arm and a leg over her in a possessive gesture that made her smile.

"I really want you to stay, Darla. This feels so right, and I can't imagine not trying to see this through."

The sincerity in his voice was enough to make her

promise him anything in that moment. Some small shred of reason held her back, barely. "I try not to make major life decisions without pants on," she joked, "but it feels right to me too."

Staying in Vegas with Jackson wasn't the life she'd planned, but maybe some plans were meant to be broken. Had there ever been another man in her life who'd made her so happy? She knew none of her past boyfriends had recognized her strengths like Jackson did or made her feel capable. With him, she felt like her life was full of possibilities instead of limits.

She needed to sleep on it to be sure, but it was hard to relax enough when the thought of a life with him had her giddy.

Chapter Twenty-One

Sizzling onions filled the kitchen with the scent of more meals than Jackson could count. It smelled like his first cooking lesson, a skill left to languish when time was tight and there were so many faster options available. But that first lesson—the first step to making any meal—would never be forgotten.

First put olive oil in a pan with onions, then figure out what you're making. His mother had given the same lesson to his sister a few years later, but it had stuck with her better. There was some sort of centering magic in it, tying him to the exact moment he was in while drawing up a thousand different comforting memories. It was just what he needed for what he was about to do.

"Huh. I guess the rumors are true."

Jackson took his eyes off the cutting board, his knife stilling. Standing in the doorway of the kitchen was Darla's roommate wearing nothing but his boxers. Jealousy crackled like water thrown on hot oil, but it dissipated just as quickly. They were roommates, nothing more.

Darla had corrected him about his name just last night, but damn if Jackson could remember it. Brian? Brandon? Something like that.

"What rumors?"

"You and Darla are sleeping together."

Jackson scraped the slices of sausage off the cutting board into the pan. He could be forgiven if he'd taken a few shortcuts and used hash browns out of the freezer, couldn't he? "I don't think what's happening between us is any of your business unless Darla decides to share it with you."

Brandon grinned. "The rumors about you are true, too."

Irritation was bunching up his shoulders in knots, and he wished he had something more to chop. "Do you have something to say?"

"Do you know they call you Doctor Ice?"

Jackson scoffed quietly at the nickname. "That's unfortunate. I sound like a rejected Batman villain."

The doorway to Darla's room opened and she stepped out, rubbing sleep from her eyes. She didn't have her glasses on yet and her hair was an unbrushed tumble around her head. Unlike her roommate, she'd put on some clothes before stumbling out, though. Her pajamas were light blue, covered in stethoscopes. Something like that had to be a gift. No one would buy it to wear, would they? On second thought, Darla might. Coming from her, it seemed more endearing than silly.

"That smells so good. What are you making?"

"Some sort of…skillet meal?" Jackson waved his spatula at the pan. "Onions, peppers, sausage and potatoes. I figured drugging ourselves with fat and carbs might help make the day a little less nerve wracking."

"What's so nerve-wracking about the day?" Brandon snatched a piece of sausage from the pan and popped it into his mouth. Seconds later he spat it out into the sink. "God, that's hot."

"Things that are frying usually are." Darla shooed him out of her way so she could get closer to Jackson.

Grateful for her nearness, he slipped an arm around her waist. "Could we talk privately?"

Brandon huffed. "Fine, just kick me out of my own kitchen."

Jackson turned off the heat to the pan and waited for Brandon to leave before he spoke again. "When does your mom's flight arrive?"

"About noon and then I've got a shift starting at three."

He considered how long it would take her to drive from McCarren Airport to UMC. There'd be little spare time, except possibly at the hospital, and he couldn't fathom having this conversation there. It was too public and made him feel too exposed.

"So you're not going to be able to make McGaffey's retirement party?" He tightened his arm around her, hoping he could enjoy that feeling many more times to come. "It's at one."

"I don't know. Maybe I'll be able to make the tail end of it."

"I've got a meeting with the chief this afternoon, so I'll probably miss some of the party too." He braced himself. "With McGaffey retiring, there's a new tenured position opening at the med school. He'd offered me his recommendation before."

"Yeah, I remember you mentioning the position. Do you think you lost his recommendation?"

He had to hope the smile he gave her didn't look as pained as it felt. "Pretty sure I did. He wanted me to prove myself as your mentor to earn it."

She sucked her breath in through her teeth, eyes closing for a moment. "I'm sorry."

Her reaction was better than he'd expected. "It's not your fault. I mean, not entirely. We both took the risk."

"It seems like the risk is bigger on your part."

He shrugged. The firing threat had been from his issues with Mevlyn, and he couldn't blame his reactions there on her. She hadn't known about him working to get Singh's recommendation either. "No, you've got risk. I told you before they usually transfer somebody in situations like ours."

She drew back from him, head cocked curiously. "If I stay here, I might be transferred?"

He took a deep breath and nodded. When they'd discussed the policy the first time, it had just been hypothetical. The reality—and accompanying guilt—sickened him. He divided the skillet up between two plates, buying himself a few more seconds to gather his thoughts. Unfortunately, it felt more like trying to grasp handfuls of sand. What had seemed so clear and easy the night before was now difficult, daunting.

"It wouldn't be a terrible thing, would it?" The question was as much for his own guilt as reassuring her. A transfer to another department might finally make her reevaluate what she wanted and the kind of risks she'd been taking. Maybe he'd even be helping her in the long run. "You could do something that isn't such a strain on your body."

All of the possibilities he saw in Darla's eyes suddenly died. Her spine went straight, her jaw set. "What?"

"You've just started your residency, so you could do anything you wanted." His words came out in a rush, as if he could speak fast enough to outrace her distrust. She was brilliant. She had to see the sense in what he was saying. "Something that would give you more downtime. Something that's better for your heart—"

"You don't know what's better for my heart," she interrupted. "You're not even a cardiologist."

"I know, but less of a strain would be good for you. There are so many potential complications."

"*Rare* complications. What is and is not good for my heart is between me and my doctor," she snapped. "Did you tell Singh about us just to get me out of trauma?"

Was that really what she thought of him? He knew he'd made some mistakes, but at the very least he thought she'd realize he wasn't being malicious. "That was the last thing on my mind, Darla. I'm just trying to find the bright side here."

"A bright side that involves me losing everything I worked for, and you getting what you want. How convenient." Her fork hit the plate with a very final sounding *clunk*. "What do I gain here?"

He closed his eyes to block out the accusation in her face, dragging his hands through his hair. The memory of her collapsing replayed over again in his head. Everything that was her, all of her future, could just cease to exist in a moment like that. All it would take was her heart being pushed too hard. Or another fainting episode without someone to catch her before her head cracked on the floor. She'd watched patients die who'd just been living their lives. Didn't she see he only wanted her safe?

"You gain a safer career," he said at last.

"That's not your call." There was a faint tremor to her voice. He couldn't tell if it was from rage or threatening tears. "Have you been planning this ever since you heard about my heart?"

"I…" His mind raced. He'd first brought up her talent with young patients early on. That had been before she told him about her heart, hadn't it? But he'd been worrying about her ever since. "No, there wasn't a plan."

"At least there's that." She crossed her arms under her breasts as her eyes bored holes into him. That probably ruled out tears. "I'd hoped you at least trusted me to make my own decisions."

"I *do* trust you. I just…" He looked down at his hands as if they held some answer, but they were empty. *He* was empty. "Is it so terrible that I like the idea of you being safe?"

"If that's what you want, you're never going to be happy with anyone." Her laugh was short and bitter. "I need you to go now."

The worry and guilt that had been twisting his stomach into knots melted away in the heat of her anger. It was almost a relief as it pushed back the worst-case scenarios running through his mind. She'd rather kick him out than consider things from his point of view. "Oh come on. This is stupid, Darla. Do you even want to go into trauma? You're putting yourself at risk to try to prove a point."

"And if I decide to go into pediatrics, it's going to be because it was my decision. Not because somebody got me forced out of trauma." She walked to grab his jacket from the hook by the front door, then threw it at him. "Get out."

"Would you just listen to me? Trauma's too dangerous for you."

"No." The single syllable was like a slap in the face, her voice rising sharply. "I'm sick of being told what I can't do. I'm not something broken for you to fix. This is the only life I have, and I can't let somebody else's fear control it."

He stared at her for a moment, at a loss, then felt something cold and hard take over. Fighting with her wasn't going to accomplish anything, especially not when she'd been happily planning on leaving for so long. Now he'd handed her a fine excuse to take back the promises she'd made the night before. He pulled on the jacket as he walked to the front door.

"You're risking your life just because you want to impress your mother."

There was no hint of that vulnerability in her from the first time they'd clashed. She stared back at him in unblinking defiance. "My life and my decisions aren't any of your business."

"Yeah, you've made that clear."

He slammed the door behind him and let his anger carry him out of the building. Whatever her cardiologist said, he couldn't believe she wasn't taking unnecessary risks. She was right, though. It was her life. Clearly she had no interest in sharing that life with him if she wouldn't listen. He didn't need her anyway. Hadn't he done just fine without any extra people in his life for years? Every footstep burned up another measure of his rage until he shut the door on his car.

Like a bubble bursting, the anger dissipated, leaving him lost and alone without it.

Chapter Twenty-Two

"Fuck!" The uncharacteristic expletive was punctuated with kicking a cupboard door. There was little satisfaction in it and it left Darla's foot stinging. For a second, she considered finding something else to kick or punch, security deposit be damned.

Brandon popped around the corner, all jocularity for once missing from his face. "What's wrong?"

"Dr. Jackhole's trying to keep me out of trauma." The words came out hotly except for the last, which her throat tried to close around, tears stinging her eyes.

"Oh my God," he breathed. "That's such a better nickname than Dr. Ice. I'm gonna have to remember that."

"Not the point, Brandon!"

He came closer to rest a hand on her shoulder, giving it a squeeze. "I'm sorry. What did he do?"

She shrugged off his hand. "He told the chief about us and then went on about how great it would be if I couldn't work in trauma anymore."

"Well, kind of insensitive, but you didn't think you could keep something like that a secret forever, right?" Brandon stared into the full heat of her glare for a moment. "You didn't, did you?"

"It's more complicated than that. He didn't give me a choice before he told the chief and then he acted like having my career derailed was a good thing. And last night he was trying to talk me into staying, before he ever brought up that I might get transferred. Like that wouldn't be a major factor in my decision."

"Why doesn't he want you in trauma?"

"He doesn't think it's healthy for me."

"Oh." Brandon was quiet for a moment. "What does your cardiologist think?"

She sighed. "Everything's fine for now. He doesn't think I need to limit myself so long as I'm comfortable, but of course Jackson never asked that. He just decided I'm too delicate."

"This came after you passed out and were rushed to cardiology, right?"

She didn't bother to answer Brandon. Maybe it had looked scarier from the outside. She'd been more annoyed by the experience than anything else, but she'd had years to deal with it.

He grabbed a fork from the drawer and sampled a piece of potato. "So if you wanted to stay, you know you could. I'm sure you could work something out with the chief if you explained everything. It wouldn't have to have anything to do with DeMatteo."

"I know. I'd been having second thoughts about moving,

but now…I don't want him to win."

Brandon gave her a pitying look. "Oh, yeah. Move across the country when you don't really want to, out of pure spite. That'll show him."

"You're really bad at this comforting thing."

"You don't need comforting." He turned the stove back on and opened the fridge. "I'm gonna cook some eggs to go with this potato and sausage stuff. Want some?"

She crossed her arms so tightly they ached. "He cooked that."

"He did, and a pig died for that sausage. Do you want that pig to have died in vain, Darla? Do you really want that on your conscience?"

Despite her best efforts, she could feel herself smiling, tears now drying. "No."

"Good answer. As I was saying, you don't need comfort. You need perspective."

"And you're the one to give it to me?"

"God no. You've got to give it to yourself. What do you want?"

"I don't know." She sank onto one of the stools around the kitchen island, rubbing her temples. "To make my mom proud, I guess."

"Okay, so. Imagine your mom is dead."

She froze, staring at him in horror. "Jesus, Brandon. I'm really glad you're going into surgery and not psychiatry."

"Work with me here, okay? Your mom is dead, or a vegetable, or just the living embodiment of pride itself. Nothing you can do will change how she feels. It's irrelevant. Now what do you want?"

"To be happy."

"And what would make you happy?"

A flutter of panic rushed through her, like a black hole of dread through her chest, inevitably sucking everything into it. "I don't know."

"What makes you happy right now?"

She breathed deep, rubbing her palm against the center of her chest. "Can you get me a glass of water? I haven't taken my pill yet." Once she had washed down the beta-blocker and given herself a moment to think, the answers came more easily. "You. My other friends. My career. Learning new things. Saving lives. Going out and having fun. Normal stuff."

"Normal stuff that's all here in Vegas."

"Well, yeah." All things Jackson had gotten her thinking about the night before, except she couldn't trust anything he said now.

What was there in Chicago, other than her mother? She had few friends growing up. Those relationships she did have had been reduced to long-distance phone calls and Facebook comments. Instead, she'd formed a new family in Nevada.

Darla gave Brandon a hopeful look. "You're planning on remaining here, aren't you?"

"That's my plan."

Getting through McCarren International Airport had never been anything short of a nightmare. The roads leading into, out of, and through the airport were like twisted knots of spaghetti. As soon as she'd finished breakfast and showered, Darla had left for the airport, reasoning that the extra money she might pay in the short term parking lot would be worth avoiding the stress of driving through the passenger pickup bay. When the board showed her mother's flight was delayed by over an hour, she was grateful she hadn't tried to make things quick.

The baggage claim felt like a cavernous pit with advertisements for different shows leering down from the second level above. Darla found a spot beside a baggage carousel to sit down and read while she waited. All around her were people reuniting, relieved to have made it through their flights. Occasionally a snippet of conversation would catch her attention, but mostly it all melted together into the sounds of a herd of humanity.

"Darla?"

She looked up from the tablet and gave her mother a relieved smile. "Hey! How was your flight?"

They hugged and Darla was reminded of how childlike her mother always made her feel, through no fault of her own. Her mother was about half an inch shorter than her, but outweighed her by twenty pounds and possessed a physical presence that commanded respect.

"Terrible. One of the other passengers was having chest pains, and we had to stop the plane in Tulsa. He should be all right, at least. There wasn't anyone else on the flight who had medical training, either."

"At least he had a good nurse like you."

Her mother waved that off with an annoyed expression. "There was hardly anything for me to do except keep him calm."

Darla smiled sadly as a memory resurfaced. "Sometimes

that's the best medicine we can offer."

"Really? That doesn't sound like you at all."

"I've been learning a lot." She slid her tablet into her purse, then fiddled with the strap a moment. "Do you have any checked luggage?"

"One bag. Are you in a rush?"

"No, it's fine. There's a retirement party at the hospital for someone, but I didn't think I'd make it anyway."

"If it's a retirement party, it's hardly important for you to go. It's not like someone quitting can help your career."

Was this how her mother had always been? She knew it was, and yet it felt like she was seeing her mother with fresh eyes. Always pushing to get ahead, always focused on the future instead of reflecting on the past. It must have been so hard for her raising Darla all alone. Why would she want to focus on anything but the future?

"I didn't want to go to help my career." She chose the words with care, speaking softly so it didn't come across argumentative. "I just happened to really like that surgeon."

"Is this the surgeon who's been mentoring you? DeMatteo?"

"No, this is McGaffey. DeMatteo is much younger. He's only a few years older than me. He's just...really good." In more ways than she could ever tell her mother.

An alarm sounded as the carousel began rotating slowly. The first few bags came out in a jumble together, then more methodically one at a time after. Her mother grabbed the sixth bag and slung her carry-on over the handle before she began wheeling it away.

"I'll be so happy when you finally come home. I hate going so long without seeing you."

Hearing that made Darla freeze, startled. "Really?"

"Of course. Don't you think I miss you?"

"I…yeah, I guess." Chicago hardly felt like home any more. The guilt of that suddenly weighed down on her.

Brandon's sarcastic comment about making choices based on spite popped into her head again and she blinked, shocked as she realized how right he was. Not just about moving to spite Jackson, but so many other decisions in her life.

"I don't want to be a trauma surgeon." She blurted the words out almost before thinking them, then cringed.

Her mother looked at her as if she'd just sprouted a second head. "You don't?"

"No, I don't. I really love research, and trauma's okay, but it's not the kind of thing that gets me excited. There's a lot of amazing research done in pediatric medicine at the UMC Children's Hospital, and I know that they're going to have space for me if I wanted to do my residency there and I think I'd want to, but it doesn't feel as sexy and cool as trauma medicine. Plus I always feel like people are talking down to me every time they bring it up, like they think I have to go into pediatrics just because I'm a woman and then I'm all, you know, fuck you, I do what I want. Except then I'm not actually doing what I want, I'm just doing what they don't want me to do." Darla stopped to gulp breath, certain her face had to be bright red after saying all of that. She'd even sworn at her mother! Well, not *at* her, but in front of her, at least.

Her mother raised one eyebrow. "Have you been saving all those words for the past twenty-six years?"

She cleared her throat. "Some of it."

"Well." Anita Morales frowned for a moment then shrugged. "If you want to go into pediatric research, that's what you should do."

Darla adjusted her glasses with one finger, as if her sight could have had any impact on her hearing. "It is?"

"Of course. Did you think I wanted you to do things you didn't want to do?" Her mother scoffed and put her hands on her hips. "Really, you actually thought that? Darla, I've been pushing you because I thought this was what you wanted. I was trying to be encouraging. If it's not what you want, then don't do it."

"Oh." Darla deflated a little. The lack of an argument was almost a letdown.

"But from all that, it doesn't sound like you want to come home either." There was no question in the statement, just a flat declaration that couldn't be argued with. The two of them locked eyes, and Darla felt a knife twist in her heart at the hurt in her mother's eyes.

"I want to make this my home." The words were soft, difficult to push out.

Her mother's arms wrapped around her to pull her into a fierce hug. She was stiff at first with surprise, then relaxed into the embrace. Just like when she was a child, her mother's hair had that scent of disinfectant to it that should have been anything but the comfort it symbolized.

"I don't know what I'll do without you," Anita said.

"We can take trips and visit and you could even move out here because they always need more experienced nurses and it doesn't have to be terrible, Mama. The past few weeks have been really good for me. I feel like…like a butterfly fresh out of the cocoon."

Her mother gave her a teary-eyed smile. "You do look beautiful. I like what you've done with your hair."

Darla automatically patted at her curls, feeling a twinge of self-consciousness, then shook her head. "Thanks, but I meant more like I'd suddenly learned how to fly."

"Well. Flying is all well and good, but you've got other things to learn, too. We have a test to prepare you for."

The words were all no-nonsense and could even sound a little cold, but Darla took them in the spirit intended and only felt loved.

Chapter Twenty-Three

The cake for the retirement party had clearly been designed to be cheery. It had also clearly failed. A lopsided yellow smiley face beamed up at Jackson with the words "Happy Retirment" beneath it. Jackson's hand itched for a tube of icing to add the missing "e", but no one had one and the mistake hadn't been noticed at the bakery. He hoped it tasted better than it looked.

Elizabeth McGaffey chuckled beside him. "Oh dear. That's really quite fitting for a retiring professor, isn't it?"

He gave her a weak smile. "And I suppose the smiley face is for retiring from surgery. Doesn't it make you want to get a scalpel and fix it?"

"Hm, no. That seems like it would fall under plastics. If they put raspberries between the layers like I asked I could see about doing something if it loses too many units."

Jackson was quiet for a moment. That look in Darla's eyes when she shut him out had been haunting him ever since he left her apartment. "It won't be the same here without you."

"I think you'll be surprised by how little the place changes in my absence. Hospitals have an equilibrium that's hard to push off course. Someone else will become the new McGaffey and things will continue on."

"No such thing as a new McGaffey."

"Of course there is. I'm still hoping it'll be you."

"I doubt it will be. I've really fucked up."

Jackson turned to lean against a table in the lounge. A few people had trickled in and out so far, but no real crowd had gathered, which was typical for these sorts of things, he'd found. Those who were available would come in when the cake was cut, a speech might be given, and that would be it for the most part. Thirty-five years of her life at the same hospital and all she'd get would be a few hungry people slipping in to steal her cake. What had seemed like the pinnacle of a career to him before now just left him feeling disgusted.

McGaffey's brow furrowed with concern. "What have you done?"

"Possibly messed up Darla's career and then told her it was a good thing. The chief wasn't going to give me his recommendation unless I could keep her here in trauma, but I don't even care about that part any more. I thought I did, but it doesn't matter. All that matters is that she's leaving, and I'm an idiot."

"Did you tell her you're in love with her?"

He winced. "Is it that obvious?"

"People don't usually get this upset over people they don't care about. It was an easy guess." She opened a bottle of water to take a sip from it, then settled herself neatly into a chair. Her glasses were low on her nose so she could watch him over their edge, making him feel like a clueless med student all over again. "You can't control what other people decide, Jackson. You know that old saying about how if you love someone, you'll let them go?"

He sighed, nodding. "And if they don't come back, they were never yours to begin with? Is that what you're telling me?"

"God, no. I was just going to point out that it doesn't matter if you love someone or not. You have to let *everyone* go, unless you plan on chaining them up in your basement."

He laughed in spite of himself. "Okay, point made. I don't have control over this."

"No, you don't. You can tell her you love her and you can do everything you can to make sure she's happy with her decision, but that's all you can do. And all you can do with the chief is your job. You do it well, and we all see that. If he doesn't, there's nothing you can do to force him to. All we have control over is ourselves, and then, only if we're lucky."

"That sounds brutally fatalistic."

"You're damn right it is." She hit her cane on the floor for emphasis. "Life's a fatal condition, Jackson. If you haven't figured that out by now, I never taught you anything."

He sighed. "If this is supposed to be a pep talk, I don't think it's working."

"It's something I should have said to you a long time ago. Especially after Amy."

For once, the name didn't make him flinch. Regret and sadness were still there, hovering in the background, but they didn't overwhelm him. "What does this have to do with her?"

"It wasn't your fault, Jackson. You had nothing to do with her getting hit, but you did give her a lot of happiness before she died. That's all anyone can ask."

"Are you telling me I just need to accept that I'm losing Darla and this promotion?"

"No, I don't know how things are going to turn out, but I do know that you can't control everything. You can't control the board or Darla or if you're going to choke to death on a ham sandwich tomorrow. Do what you can and accept the rest."

He bowed his head, but nodded. "I'm trying."

The chief stepped in, frowned at the cake, and then focused on Jackson. "DeMatteo, do you have a minute?"

"Yeah, I do."

As he walked past McGaffey, the older woman gave him a meaningful look. "It's a fatal condition. Make it count."

Outside in the hall, the chief led him away in the direction of his office. "What's fatal? Should I be worried?"

"No, she was just talking about life."

In the chief's office, Singh shut the door, then took a seat across the desk from him. As pessimistic as McGaffey's talk had been, he found himself strangely comforted by it. The nervousness he expected to feel as he looked at the chief failed to materialize.

"Setting aside what we discussed yesterday, how have things been going with Morales?"

It was the question he'd been dreading and of course it had to be the first one out of the chief's mouth. Jackson leaned back in his chair and cast a look toward the ceiling, as if some answer would be delivered from heaven for him. But there was nothing to be done but be honest.

"Great, as far as the work goes. She has some rough spots, but that's all to be expected with a first-year resident. She's intelligent, passionate, seems to have a real knack for surgery and once she got settled in she has nerves of steel." He swallowed, preparing for the next part. "But I do think her strengths might lie more in pediatrics than trauma."

The chief frowned. "Are you driving another intern off or is this your recommendation for transferring her?"

"No. This has nothing to do with me. I've done everything a good mentor is supposed to do, including identifying her strengths and guiding her toward them. What she decides from here is up to her. To try to control her choice is..." He trailed off, shaking his head. "It was a shitty deal from the start, Chief."

"You think my suggestions are shitty?" His expression was unreadable. Was that controlled fury in his eyes or cool detachment?

The impulse to lie and try to work things in his favor rose, but Jackson pushed it aside. That was what Dick would do. "In this case, yeah, I do."

Singh was quiet for a moment. The only sound in the office was the steady tapping of his pen against the edge of his desk. "That's quite a thing to say considering some of your poor choices recently."

"You want someone who'll lie and kiss your ass? Get Dick on the tenure track, then. I don't want to do that. Yeah, some of my students fail out of my classes and a lot of interns don't want to work with me, because I make it hard. I don't shield them from the fact that people will die if they make the wrong choices. Some people can't deal with that. Better to figure that out while they're learning than when someone's life is actually in their hands." He leaned forward slightly. "But the students who pull through my classes? Those are the ones with fellowships now. Those are the ones who pushed themselves to find their own excellence, and I don't know if they would have pushed that hard if I didn't make them."

"I see." The chief made a note on a pad of paper and Jackson felt his heart sink.

The lack of reaction was likely a bad sign, but what was there to be done about it? As McGaffey had said, he couldn't force the chief to see what he didn't want to see. He raked a hand through his hair, taking a deep, calming breath.

"You know having a relationship with an intern wouldn't make you look good to the board if they knew."

"Maybe people will finally believe me now when I tell them I don't think I'm perfect." He shrugged. "But it's over anyway. If anyone has to suffer for it, I'd still prefer it be me. She doesn't deserve having her reputation harmed."

"I see." Another note on that damned paper. "So what do you think your biggest weakness is?"

His eyes rolled before he could stop himself. Half a dozen cliché answers for such a cliché question came to mind, but there was only one honest one. "I'm a control freak who's always trying to fix everything."

Singh chuckled, nodding. That unreadable of his mask finally slipped. "You are, but you've finally come clean. I think ensuring you and Morales don't work together again should be fine. You're right that she doesn't deserve to suffer for it."

Nothing about removing her from trauma. Just his service. At least she couldn't blame him for that. He breathed a bit easier, nodding. "Thank you."

"And I'm sorry for giving you such a hard time over this, but I had to be sure no one could argue I was playing favorites. They all know how much I admire you."

The meaning of his words sank in. Jackson laughed as well, relief loosening up the tension that had been locked around his rib cage for far too long. "You do? I never would have guessed."

"You're good at what you do, DeMatteo, and I think you've gotten even better over the past couple weeks. You have my recommendation."

The chief stood and Jackson joined him to shake his hand, his mind reeling. McGaffey had already spoken on his behalf to the board, which meant his promotion was nearly guaranteed. The minor increase in pay would be nice, but the change in position was of far greater importance. New opportunities would open up because of this. His long-term goals were all coming within reach.

And it all felt empty.

When it was over, what would the prestige of his career leave him with besides a badly decorated retirement cake? He'd go to an empty home, maybe see his sister and Chris once a week and work. Everyone else he loved was either dead or he'd pushed them away.

Out in the hall he made a call. It rang twice before being answered. "Hello?"

"Hey Dad. Listen, I've got some vacation time I should really use, and I was wondering about visiting you guys."

Chapter Twenty-Four

Nancy took the offered chart from Darla's hands and greeted her with a smile. "How does it feel to almost be a licensed doctor?"

"About the same as it did right after I took the test." Darla laughed a little and shook her head. "I'll finally relax when they finish processing my application."

Switching to the residency program in the children's hospital had been remarkably painless after all of Darla's worry over it. She saw less of Brandon and Maggie, but they hardly had time to socialize at work anyway. It was difficult, as she knew it would be, but satisfying. There was really only one thing she could complain about. She just couldn't shake the longing for Jackson.

Nancy nodded. "Mine took two months."

Darla groaned at the thought, closing her eyes. "Don't tell me that. The woman I spoke to said since I had everything organized properly it could take as little as two weeks. I want to believe her."

"Well…I wouldn't want to shake your faith."

Once Nancy was on her way, Darla checked the time on the wall of the residents' lounge. She had enough time to eat something and possibly even take a nap, assuming she wasn't paged for anything. Both sounded good.

"Darla."

Jackson's voice came from behind her. She hadn't been sure she'd hear him say her name again, especially not after she'd transferred to the children's hospital. All her effort to put distance between them was wasted if he didn't plan on leaving her alone.

She let another heartbeat pass without responding, giving herself time to prepare, then turned around. Jackson was standing in the doorway with his arms braced against the frame, those green eyes of his drinking her in as if his life depended on it. His eyes might as well have been his hands for all the intimacy of that look, and when his gaze finally locked with hers she shivered. He must not have been working, because he wore a pair of jeans that looked like they'd been tailored just for him. All she wanted to do was touch him again.

He'd tried to make decisions for her. He'd refused to trust her judgment. She had to remind herself of that, repeating it like a mantra in her mind to push away temptation. Drawing on her anger for strength, she squared her shoulders and raised her chin in defiance.

"Yes, Dr. DeMatteo?"

The other two residents in the lounge were listening. She could see that people out in the hall had noticed the tension between them and were staring, but staring was nothing in comparison to talking and she was sure they'd do that endlessly if she left with Jackson. Worse than that was the way her gut churned at the thought of being alone with him.

The attention didn't escape Jackson's notice either. "Could we speak privately?"

"I don't think that would be appropriate."

He paused, genuine surprise crossing his face. His lips parted to speak, then closed again. After a moment he nodded. "Then we'll speak here."

"What?" That churning in her stomach would put a washing machine to shame. She took half a step back, though there was no possible escape with him blocking the doorway.

"I'm an idiot, and I was so scared of losing you that I chased you away, but I thought I was protecting you."

She swallowed past the lump in her throat. "You were wrong."

"I know, and I'm sorry." He looked over his shoulder to the hall outside, which had grown silent. Every nurse, doctor and attendee had actually stopped to listen and stare. When he looked at her again she dearly regretted not going somewhere more private with him. "Whatever you decide to do with yourself is the right choice for you, and I hope it makes you happy, but you need to know everything before you make that choice."

She gave a small gesture around the room. "I'm pretty sure I've already made all my important choices."

"I love you."

Her heart stopped for a moment before it began again, racing this time. "What?" The single word was barely above a whisper.

"I love you. I want you happy and doing whatever feels right for you, and I never set out to push you toward anything." He finally stepped forward from the doorway and closed the distance between them to take her hands. "I can survive without you, but it's not the life I want."

"Jackson, I'm not—"

"Please let me finish before you tell me to go away," he interrupted. "I want you to have all the facts this time. When I told you to think about pediatrics, that wasn't me trying to push you out of trauma. That was just me being honest about your strengths."

She looked down at their hands, thinking that over. He couldn't have been using her as much as she feared if he was risking things that early on. "You were right."

"I'm glad. Especially since you're doing that here instead of in Chicago." He squeezed her hands, tugging her a little closer. "You make me feel alive instead of just living. I don't want to work extra hours and miss all the new movies and punish myself with shitty old cars because I'm being sensible. I want to be the person you make me feel like. Hopefully that's a person you want. I don't know. I don't have the best track record when it comes to this sort of thing."

She pursed her lips, blinking rapidly to fight back tears. Something needed to be said, but her throat felt too tight to get a word out. Instead of words, she rose up on her tiptoes to press her lips to Jackson's, letting his hands go to wrap her arms around his neck.

It took her a few seconds to find her voice, but when she did, the answers were all clear. "I'm not telling you to go away."

"You're not?"

She shook her head. Her lips brushed his with the murmured words. "And I love you, too."

"Good." He hugged her close to him and kissed her ear. "Now can we continue the rest of this conversation more privately? I hate having an audience."

Taking pity on him, she led him away to the nearest on-call room, then kissed him again as soon as the door was shut.

He sighed against her lips, one hand cupping her cheek. God, that gesture, so strong and tender—so much like the man.

"So my sister's getting married in a couple weeks," he said. "And I'm the best man. Do you want to be my date?"

She laughed softly. "Will there be dancing?"

"Until you dance through your stockings."

"All right, but then you have to do something for me."

He leaned back to give her an incredulous look. "I have to bribe you to be my date? How?"

"The next time we have a day off together, we're going to sit down and marathon through all the movies you still need to see."

He arched a brow. "I've missed a lot of movies…"

"I know. We'll only stick to the really important, really geeky ones."

He closed his eyes, shaking his head slowly before lowering himself for a kiss. "The things I do for love."

Acknowledgments

I have so much gratitude and respect for my editors, Heather Howland and Vanessa Mitchell. Thank you to my copyeditor, Mary Kate Castellani, who saved me from chronic comma neglect. That trick with the ring really does work and I learned how to do it from Dr. Simon Carley at Manchester Metropolitan University. Without my mother's input and occasionally disturbing stories, I never would have been able to bring UMC to life. My entire world changed while working on this book, but steadfast friends like Maggie and Addison kept my head on through it all. Thanks for all the support.

About the Author

A native of Southern Nevada, C.M. Stone moved to the frigid north woods of Wisconsin after college. She wrote her first book at the age of seven and and decided then and there that she would never accept any other career. Despite a lifelong love for romance novels, Cee considers herself possibly the least romantic person on earth. Luckily, her fiance more than makes up for that lack, and inspires her on a daily basis. To hear more from Cee and get updates, visit her website (www.ceeemstone.com), follow her on Twitter (@CeeEmStone), or like her on Facebook.

Discover the Gambling Hearts series...

ONE NIGHT IN VEGAS

Eliza DeMatteo returns home knowing her matchmaking older brother wants to set her up with his best friend. But Eliza already knows enough about sexy cowboy Chris Yerrick, the man who crushed her heart when they were kids. Still, there's no reason they can't enjoy New Year's Eve together, even if the fireworks between them burn hotter than the Vegas Strip. But this time, what doesn't happen in Vegas could haunt them forever...

www.ingramcontent.com/pod-product-compliance
Lightning Source LLC
Chambersburg PA
CBHW030312200626
46816CB00002BA/875